ALGOMA COLLEGE LIBRARY

copyright © 1974 George Ryga

published with assistance from the Canada Council

Talonbooks
201 1019 East Cordova
Vancouver
British Columbia V6A 1M8
Canada

This book was typeset by Linda Gilbert of B.C. Monthly Typesetting Service, designed by David Robinson and printed by Web Offset for Talonbooks.

Second printing: October 1977

Canadian Shared Cataloguing in Publication Data

Ryga, George, 1932—
   Hungry hills

  ISBN 0-88922-134-0 pa.

  I. Title.
  PS8585.Y393H85   C813'.5'4
  PR9199.3.R

Hungry Hills

a novel by George Ryga

one

The faded board swinging in the wind said "Elsie's Coffee Shop & Eats." I could have drunk a river, I was that dry, so I entered.

I dropped my bag inside the door and looked around. All the tables were littered with crumbs of food and coated with the same grey dust I could taste between my teeth. One table near me seemed less soiled than the others, and I sat at it.

Elsie didn't know me. Three years is a long time, although I remembered her very well. The cop had stopped for a drink and bought me a sandwich then — a sandwich of stale bread with bits of leathery chicken inside it.

She hadn't changed. Still the same mountain of woman with a dirty white apron cutting into the folds of her stomach where it tied, and the same brown dress, bleached down her sides from the sweat of her armpits. The wart on her thick upper lip was crowned with the sprig of dark hair I remembered. She stood, watching me with a vacant, hostile stare — the back of her head propped against the mirror which covered a considerable portion of the wall behind the counter. I stared back at her, remembering.

Three years ago, Corporal Kane and the welfare man had stopped here. We sat at a table further in — the furniture was rearranged since, but then there was a table in that corner. I sat between them, facing the street. The windows were just as dirty then as now, and the weather as hot.

"What you got for your boy friend to drink?" Kane half-hollered at Elsie. Her big face got red, and she scratched under a breast with her thumb.

"I don't got no boy friend," she said thickly. Corporal Kane slapped his knee and laughed — that heavy laugh of his which ends up in a girlish squeal, and sounds crazy coming from a big guy like him.

The welfare man, a Mr. Webber, or Webster — can't remember now, because he was one of those people you don't remember by name — had grey hair and a small grey-black moustache, and he didn't speak much. When my knee brushed against his, he moved away in the car, because he wore a new brown suit which had such a press in the pants you could cut your finger on the crease. And I was pretty dirty.

Elsie sighed and moved away from the mirror. She fished around under the counter and came towards me, holding a moist cloth in her hand.

First she picked up the full ash-tray from the table in front of me, and emptied it into another, equally full, at the next table. Then she wiped it clean with the cloth. Using the same cloth, she wiped my table. When she finished, the table had the smell of stale tobacco ashes and soap.

"Wot ya want?"

Her voice sounded like it started in her stomach and came up through a towel in her throat.

"A coffee ice-cream."

"Ya go to hell!" Her face was still flat, but her eyes were getting angry. She turned her face away from me and stared out into the dusty street.

Nothing much had changed. The broken window of the hardware store across the road was fixed since I last was here. The bank next door had a new sign out — "Imperial Bank of Canada" it read — but the building was still the same as when Stanley Muller operated his blacksmith shop within its walls. So the new sign reminded me of new shoelaces on a bleached old pair of boots.

Folks had funny stories to tell about Stanley Muller — he came from Poland or Germany, and never learned to speak English too well. After five years in Canada, he tried to get his citizenship papers. At his court hearing, he was so nervous, what little English he knew he lost.

"Your name?" the magistrate had asked.

"Blacksmith," Stanley had said.

"Your occupation?"

"Muller."

Everyone laughed. Even the magistrate smiled.

Yet Muller might have become part of my family if he'd lived long enough. Maybe I'd have been able to move into town with him, away from the hills. But all that is gone now.

Another summer, hot and dusty as every summer I remembered. The same strong, hot wind. Here in town, it came past the grain elevator down the wide open street, carrying fine sand and a litter of paper and dead leaves, which it brushed across the dirty window of Elsie's coffee shop with a delicate scratching sound. I watched, and saw a large grey cat with a lame hind leg appear from the narrow space between the bank and the hardware store, and cross the street toward the café. The wind raised the fur high on his back, giving him a lethal appearance, which his sticky, tired eyes belied.

"How long's it been since the last rain?" I asked.

"Ya want somethin', or ya just aimin' to rest, goddamn you!" Elsie suddenly turned and planted her beefy red hands on the table before me. Her eyes were watering with anger, and her voice had become quite crisp and strong.

I only had coffee ice-cream once — Pete made some for me. I liked it, because it left a nice, lingering taste in my mouth long after I had eaten it. But . . .

"I'll have a Coke."

Elsie waddled away to the cooler, and returned shortly with the drink in a bottle, which she thumped down hard on the table. This violent handling made it fizz and run over, making a dirty brown puddle on the table-top around the bottom of the bottle. I was fascinated with this mess, and tipped the bottle back and forth, enjoying the sucking, snapping sound I made breaking the surface tension of the liquid.

"Hey! Cut that out! Yo're givin' me a headache doin' that!"

Elsie had retreated behind the counter into the same posture and place at the mirror that she held when I first entered the café. She was getting salty.

I wondered if all women without men suffer the same way. My Aunt Matilda was one long headache after Muller went his way. I couldn't scratch in the same room she happened to be in without giving her a headache. A spoon dropping, or a board banging in the wind, and she'd dig her fingers into her hair and press like her head was a lemon from which she was squeezing juice.

What would she be like now?

Soon, I would be seeing her again. Yet until this moment I hadn't thought of what sort of person I would meet. Would she know me now? I was big — fully grown, and I knew everything I had to know. I stared at the Coke bottle and tried so hard to remember. Her voice — her face — these I recalled well. But I had lost the feel of her — the separate sounds and shadows of a presence. She had travelled a long way on her strange, confusing road.

A hard, dry, tight-lipped woman my Aunt Matilda was, with narrow hips and the thin, bone-hard arms of a boy. The skin on her neck and face was mottled by brown specks, like the speckled shell of some chicken eggs.

"Too much sun she gets," my mother used to say in that jealous way of hers. "If she washed herself in skimmed milk every second day, she'd soon get rid of that."

My mother had opinions, but no audience, for she was tuberculous and confined indoors most of the time. Which was unfortunate, for I remember her as a gentle, bewildered person with wonderful bursts of fun in a retiring, hungry existence. But the law of our household gave authority only to those who worked in the fields, and so Aunt Matilda was always the dominant one of the two women.

One summer Aunt Matilda took up with Stanley Muller, the blacksmith. It was ten miles from our farm to town, but Aunt Matilda walked, sometimes four nights in a row, returning with the first glow of sun in the mornings. She was tired, hot and happy, and would begin her daily chores without breakfast.

"Aunt Matilda's been gone all night. Don't she sleep?" I used to ask my mother.

"Sure she's slept — with her back to the coal sacks, for she ain't that strong or big!" my mother would reply, then she would laugh and slap her knee with her thin hand.

One Sunday, Stanley Muller came to visit us and eat dinner at our table. He had something wrong with his chest, for his breath sang like an organ. And he had black pocks on his forehead and nose, where fragments of flying coal and steel dust had imbedded deeply in his skin. He sat next to my aunt, on a bench which was too small for them, and they wriggled much to keep their seats.

"Ven you have to sharpen ploughshares, bring dem to me. Stanley do for noting." Muller spoke to my father, who shyly lowered his head over his plate. Then Muller ate, his large hand enclosing all but the prongs of his fork. I remember watching him cut meat with the edge of the fork, and butter his bread by drawing the prongs lengthwise across the slice, which produced a lovely, rippled design. I wanted to do the same thing, but when I reached for the butter dish with my fork, mother caught me by the wrist and drew my hand back.

Aunt Matilda walked some way with Muller when he left that evening. When she returned, my mother and father were having tea, and she joined them.

"What you want to take up with a guy like him for?" Mother chided. "He don't even speak English good."

My aunt picked her teeth with her thumbnail and looked at my mother thoughtfully. But she didn't say anything.

Strong as he was, Stanley Muller died that summer. The story went that he had a drink of cold water while he was hot at his anvil, and the drink gave him a chill to his chest. For two weeks he lay on his straw cot. Aunt Matilda took food to him, but he would not eat. The front of his smithy was open, and farmers came, bringing ploughshares and axes for him to sharpen. But he never relit the fire in his forge.

Now they have made a bank of his building.

"How much better if it had been me instead of him!" Aunt Matilda cried at the burial of Muller. My mother hushed her to be still, and father wrung his hands and glanced over his shoulder to see how many of the neighbours heard.

It was a terrible thing of my aunt to say — young as I was then, I felt the full weight and pain of her words. And as I watched them shovelling the earth over Muller, I was numb with despair.

So much I could now remember of Aunt Matilda in love — how she would surprise me by grabbing at my arm and pulling me to press tightly against herself. Sometimes I would come into the house and find her kneading her thin lips as she studied her face in a broken sliver of mirror. When I cleared my throat to make my presence known to her, she would giggle and shoo me off with a wave of her hand.

"Run away and do something! You're worse than your father used to be!"

After the tragedy of Muller's death, she sort of caved in on herself and didn't laugh any more. Her face got thin and old, and I remember how her hair started to grey. Our house was small and thin-walled. At nights, I often heard her crying in her bed and tossing from side to side.

My father became worse — he took to talking to himself, and our home became an angry, nervous place.

I began straying from home, not wanting to go back even for food. Some days, I would just walk down the road past Whittles' store, until I got tired. Other days, I would visit one of the many farms up and down the road from us. There were always kids to play with — there were more kids in the countryside than hogs and cattle put together — kids big and small, lame and straight, all sitting in the sun, waiting for something to do.

I kept leaving our place because there was nothing to do at home. Nobody cared if I dressed or washed, and I was never shown how to do chores. Now my aunt and my mother changed for the worse. With my father, it didn't matter.

"Go ask Jim to split some wood, and I'll bake bread." My mother rose from bed one afternoon, hot-faced and wheezing, and spoke to my aunt.

"I'll get it myself," Aunt Matilda said testily. "Your Jim would water the garden on a rainy day!"

Mother didn't argue. She merely went back to bed, and remained there until the following day. Her everlengthening spells in bed did not disturb me then. I was really pleased, for when she was wakened during the day, she would rise blue with meanness and demand to know why she could not be left in peace. If she woke by herself late in the afternoon, she was peevish about being allowed to sleep the day away. As for my father — memories of him had always been dim. A mild man, with down-bent head and repentant eyes — afraid of folks, and avoiding even us.

But there is no pity among the poor.

One afternoon, I strayed further than usual — over to the Hardy's place. There were two boys and a smaller girl — nice kids to play with, for they didn't call me names. We tore around through the yard and out into the fields, where we upset the cows enough to make them move away from us. Fred Hardy, the father of the family, whistled to us, and we saw him wave at us to come in. We were all hungry, and ran a race to see who would get to the house first. The two boys beat me, and their sister was left some distance behind. When the boys reached the door, they squeezed past their father and went in. I started to follow, but was stopped by Mr. Hardy's hand catching me at the neck.

"Ya plannin' to eat, then stay all night?" he growled at me. "Go home, ya little bugger!"

So I went home. It had always been the same — even when my father lived, I had nobody to take my part. The bone of the outcast stuck in my throat all through childhood.

"Look at him, will ya! He ain't afraid of the night! He's got the heart of a thief — even looks like a thief! Just look at his eyes, and the way his teeth stick out. Isn't that a thief if ya ever seen one?"

"The way he fights, too. Tore my kid's lip to here, when he was called a little pig for not washing his face."

This was when the neighbourhood went out of its way to pick on me. At best, they were no meaner than Mr. Hardy had been. But I was a boy, and when I became lonely, I would go to peoples' homes uninvited. I didn't leave until I was asked to or told to go home.

Yet it wasn't something I understood then, and I was happy despite it all. I still am, for what difference would it make if I wasn't? Who would hear me?

After Muller's death, my aunt and I grew more distant, for she was also beginning to die, as I was coming to life. We never came together, yet there were moments when I came close to invading her world, as she must have invaded mine without my being aware of her.

One night, I had overstayed at someone's house, and was ordered home when the children were called in for bed. I went out on the road, kicked dust about with my bare feet. The earth and sky were still grey with twilight. When darkness fell, I began making my way home. The road I took led past the cemetery — and as I neared the burial ground, the early moon rose, silvering the grass and dusty road with a soft, comforting light.

I had no fear of the cemetery, for I had no misfortunes with it any more peculiar than I might have had with a pasture field. Also, I was spared the terrifying tales wiser adults sometimes improvise for children in a closer family than mine. Anyway, as I neared the cemetery, I heard a voice, and stopped to listen. Yes — I heard it again, coming from behind the willow hedge which bordered the grounds.

I was curious, and crouching low, I tiptoed off the road and up to the hedge. Pushing aside the willow branches, I peered through.

There, clear and sharp in the moonlight, was my Aunt Matilda, lying on top of Stanley Muller's grave. She was so near I could have spoken to her. She was lying on her stomach over the grave, her cheek pressed into the mound and turned away from me.

She held her kerchief in her hand, and waved it frantically up and down. She was saying something — something pleading and sad in the cooing tones of a pigeon. I got scared and chilly, and moved away towards the road. Then I ran all the way home. . . .

"Did you know my Aunt Matilda?" I asked, and Elsie stirred her massive bulk. She gave me a mean look, then turned her attention back to the windy street outside the café.

"Wot?"

Leaving a dime on the table, I got up without tasting the Coke she had brought me. I no longer had any stomach for refreshments. So near to home again, and a hot excitement had begun to creep through me.

It was late afternoon now, but the sun still burned like a furnace. The wind from the hills was good, even though it was full of smells of hot leaves and parched grey earth. It was all so familiar — the smell of home — all a part of other summers I remembered; hot sun, dry winds, and a thirst which only a great rain could quench.

Even from the simmering street, bordered with grey clapboard buildings, I could see the hills beyond the single grain elevator which split the landscape. How blue they were! How peaceful and silent, falling away like great abandoned anthills. Small tufts of trees and brush clung to the valleys, but the hilltops were bare, rounded and wind-blown. Beyond this first range of hills was home. There the land was flatter, and shielded by taller trees and windbreaks to make farm land from which the hardy could eke out some sort of life.

I started to cross the street, and the wind struck my chest full force, billowing my shirt out behind my back. It was a cool, pleasant sensation, for my clothes were damp with sweat and had stuck to me.

A clatter broke the silence of the street, and I turned to see a team of lathery horses appear from the corner back of the livery stable. They approached me at a fast trot. I jumped towards the bank, out of the way, and watched.

I knew the horses — Pete and Jenny, the plow nags which the Swifts owned. I looked up at the standing driver, who was lashing the animals with the tail-ends of the leads. Sure as hell! It was Johnny Swift!

"Hi! Ya goddamned, rubber-legged hammerheads! Hi!" Johnny's voice had grown stronger, but his language hadn't changed. He had been the only kid I knew who could make a dog cringe with a verbal scolding. Kids only played with Johnny Swift when there was nobody else to play with, for he was rough.

"Johnny!" I shouted.

I could see his face plainly as he neared me. Big beads of sweat stood out on his temples and cheeks, trickling to dry in the dark fuzz on his jaws. These dark streaks made him appear older than he really was. His head was uncovered, and his long hair was a wind-twisted mess. He looked up and saw me. For a moment he didn't recognize me, then suddenly he yanked hard on the reins, bringing his team to a rearing stop. Dust swirled around the wagon and rose in a thick cloud.

"Hey — Snit! Is it really you? How ya doin' boy? Goin' outa this damned town?" He shouted with pleasure, and a loose smile creased his cheeks.

I ran over to the wagon and stepping on a wheel spoke, swung myself up on the seat beside Johnny, and we were on our way. I looked back and saw the dust lifted by the wind envelop the bank building. Only the new sign showed through the cloud. This struck me as peculiar, and I giggled.

With a vicious lashing at their backs, Johnny had the horses at a gallop before we left town. The wagon jolted and bounced over the deeply rutted, dust-covered road, and I had to clutch the wooden seat with both hands to keep from falling off. Johnny was standing all the while, his filthy clothes slapping around him. I noticed his trousers were worn completely through at the seat, and on his feet he wore boots of different sizes and colours, and no socks.

When we passed the grain elevator and were out in the country, Johnny sat down and allowed the horses to break gallop into a trot.

"Good to see ya, Snit — ya rotten little bugger! How ya been, anyhow? It's been what? Three — naw, goin' on to four years since they took ya away. Whatcha come back for? This ain't no place for a man. Ya'd been better off wherever it was ya were. What'd they do — put ya in jail, or something?"

"Naw — a welfare home."

"A *welfare* home! What in hell is that?" Johnny's brows crinkled suspiciously. I grinned.

"Well, it ain't a Sunday school. More like a jail, except it got no bars across the windows."

Johnny relaxed, and brushed his sleeve awkwardly over his temples to wipe the sweat away. He also wiped off the dirt, and I marvelled at how white and soft his skin was under all that grime and filth.

"Boy! That's more like it." He sighed. "Sure wish I knew a guy who'd been to jail. Sort of makes a man outa a kid, I hear."

"What's new hereabouts?" I asked.

"Nuthin'. Same old place — same old hills. Same old two-bit farmers, and each one hungry as a bitch with a dozen pups. Nuthin's new." Johnny looked down at his feet, and seeing his mismatched boots, pulled them under the seat so I would not see. I did the same with my feet, for I wore a newish pair of black oxfords, and suddenly felt ashamed of them.

"Ya still living with yore old man?"

"Yeh," Johnny nodded. "He don't like me none, but I don't like him neither, so we get along all right."

He became quiet after this. But I felt, each time I looked away, he was watching me, trying to figure me out. Once, I glanced at him sudden-like, and caught him staring at me and my clothes. He grinned with embarrassment.

I had forgotten how a human being smells in poverty — the musty smell of sweat and old clothes, and hair and feet that don't get washed. This was the smell of Johnny — the smell of yeast and horses. I began to wonder if it wasn't all a bad mistake. Maybe I should have done what Pete suggested.

"Christ, but some folks'll be surprised to see ya come back, Snit!" Johnny laughed bitterly. "They signed a petition that long to get ya packed off — an' I know every name that went on that paper."

"I don't want to know, Johnny!" I was startled at the sharpness of my voice.

"Hey! What's eatin ya? I just wanna be friendly. Ya gonna need friends bad when ya get back, I'm tellin ya!" Johnny said peevishly, his moon-face setting hard as he turned to me.

"I'm sorry. I'm kinda beat." I was miserable. The sun burned into my eyes like two jets of a blowtorch. I bowed my head, and Johnny was silent for the rest of our drive.

Ten miles — but the ride was without end or time. It was a silent ride now. Folks in the hills don't talk much, and I was back in my hills and of my hills — I could never lose that, any more than I could lose my staggering, long-stepped country walk. You are born with these things and you never forget them. So I had been away three years, but I had no more to say to Johnny Swift than he had to say to me. I did not want to know the names of the folk who had *signed against me*, because I was not returning for revenge. I was returning with a presentable set of clothes on my back, a jacket on my arm, and a cheque in my pocket — and I was returning to live and work among my own people.

To occupy myself, I milked my thumbs and tried to recollect all I knew of Johnny Swift. I felt Johnny was still watching me, and also trying to remember.

Johnny's folks had no use for him as a kid. They figured he was too lazy and careless to amount to anything. And he was, at that. It was spoken about the neighbourhood that old Walter Swift lived by 'the Book and the axe,' and his family went to pot for it. Johnny had once told me the old man actually *did go* to bed at night with a Bible in his hand and an axe by the bedside — to accommodate the devil in case he came acalling during the dark hours. Johnny had been a dodger. When he left his spade in the potato patch and jumped the fence to go larking the rest of the day, old Walter Swift took it off on the mother for bringing the boy up wrong. She was a pious, shivery little woman who died while I was still here.

"Sadie died of a sorrow for that punk boy — God bless her!" Walter Swift had stopped by for water, which he shakily held to his lips in a dipper when he spoke.

Aunt Matilda turned red and jumped him.

"Sorrow, hell! You clubbed her to death, you goddamn animal!" she shouted. Swift never did drink his water. He threw it and the dipper back into the bucket.

"Just ya don't go cuttin' me none, Matilda Mandolin! Just ya don't go cuttin' me, ya blasted heathen bitch!" He hunched over and his hands shook like he was going to nail my aunt one. Then he turned and left our doorway.

When I told Johnny about the incident the next time I saw him, he laughed.

We were now close to home. Whittles' store stuck out of the landscape like the awkward heap of old lumber it was. As we passed, I strained to see through the soiled windows into the shop — to check against my memory the rough board shelves of dusty clothes, canned vegetables, flour bags, cattle salt, tobacco, and dried fruit. I could even remember the smell of the store now — the paper-and-grass smell of aging dry goods, strongly laced with the odour of the kerosene barrel which occupied the middle of the floor. But I could see nothing, for the sun was over the roof now, and the windows were blank and glazed like the eyes of a dead cow.

"Ya gonna stay with yore aunt?" Johnny asked. I was surprised to hear his voice after the many miles of silence between us — as I was surprised by his question. It had never occurred to me to wonder if I would stay with my aunt — I was returning home, and home was the place my aunt lived in. Now I wondered.

The farms we had passed seemed uncompromising and deserted somehow, grey and stark as the hills against which they were outlined. Almost hostile, and the further we drove in, the more uncomfortable I felt. I took my time answering Johnny, because I was no longer certain of the answer.

"Yes," I finally said.

Johnny grunted and faint lines crinkled his brow.

"She ain't been much since yore old lady went, Snit. You wouldn't know her much now — looks like a scarecrow, and acts batty as hell. Even the farm ain't much any more." I laced the fingers of my hands, and my palms felt sticky against each other.

Next would be the church, and then, a short distance off, our farm.

"Johnny," I spoke too quickly, "do you think — well, is it right for me to come back?"

"I couldn't care less. I just think yo're crazy."

"That's not what I meant. What will folks think — my aunt — will she want me back, ya think?"

Johnny thought on this for a while.

"I don't know." He squirmed as he spoke and scratched at his neck. "How can I tell what the hell folks think? Nobody's dyin' to see ya back, that I know. Folks don't like ghosts croppin' back — especially ones they ain't so sure of. But don't ask me. Go talk to Whittles — or yore aunt, if ya can get any sense outa what she says."

"What ya mean — folks ain't sure of me? Don't ya know why I'm comin' back?"

Johnny pulled the horses to a stop and looked into my face. There was suspicion in his eyes now, and a strange hostility which seemed so much a part of the hill country.

"No, I don't know why yo're comin' back," he said. "You tell me."

"I been gone a long time," I began. "I done some good things and I done some bad things. But I want to make a start somewhere — anywhere. I'm on my own now, nobody's got anything against me. The way I figured it, I may as well go back where I come from and try a fresh start there. So I hitchhiked in from Edmonton, and now I'm on yore wagon just short of home by one hill. That's all there's to it."

"Yo're comin' here — to make somethin' of yore life?" I could tell Johnny didn't believe a word of what I said. I nodded. "What ya gonna start with — yore teeth?"

"I've got some money."

"Ya think the bit of dough ya got is gonna bring rain and good times here?" Johnny laughed a hard, tight giggle. Then he laughed louder, until he clutched his stomach and bent over his knees to catch his breath. When he looked up, there were tears in his eyes, and I felt sick and frightened.

"Boy, that's the best one I heard yet!" He wiped the tears from his eyes with the back of his hand, then reached for the reins to drive on.

"Just a minute," I said, "I'm getting off now. Think I'll walk the rest of the way in.

"Suit yoreself — yo're welcome to ride, but then it's yore shoe-leather, so if ya wanna walk, then walk," Johnny said, fighting to keep a grin back. I jumped off the wagon, and he drove off, trotting his horses now. I waited until the dust he raised settled, then followed after him on foot.

The earth was hot, and soon I felt the soles of my shoes burn with the heat stored in the dusty road. I felt wretched and thirsty. Somehow, my arrival home was not what I had expected. I had forgotten the harsh cruelty of the land and its people — the desperate climate which parched both the soil and the heart of man. There were no friends here — there never would be.

Now I was returning, with clothes which somehow still remained clean and out of place. But I was returning as a burden to those with whom I had to share a place on this earth — burden to what remained of my family, and a burden to the conscience of a community which had once banished me. I had already made Johnny Swift resent me. There would be others.

I was now alongside the church. It was desolate and parched, with whitewash on the siding showing only under the eaves, where the walls were shielded from the sun and weather. The rest of the building was grey and decaying. The door sagged and was held closed by a length of rope and a peg. The windows were cracked and taped with strips of paper in grotesque patterns, like veins in the eyes of a man who has worked through a night without sleep. The churchyard was overgrown with dandelion and quack grass, and the gate had fallen and grown into the earth.

Now on a rise of the road, I could see my old home in the distance. It was desolate and grey, and I felt I could go no further. I turned into the churchyard, and making my way around the building to the shady east wall, sat down to rest. I unlaced my shoes, and removing them to ease the pressure on my swollen feet, lay back into the stringy grass.

two

I sprang to my feet in a panic, for momentarily I had no recollection of where I was. The sky overhead was a blue-black sheet, punctured by stars, and the outline of the hills was now murky and strange. I could not tell how long I had slept, or whether it was the deep twilight of evening or of morning I had wakened to. Reaching for my shoes, I brushed my hand against the grass. There was no dew.

Recollection came quickly; I remembered the afternoon and my ride with Johnny Swift. I walked around the church and onto the road. The air was warm, and heavy with the odours of dry decay. Once I was on the road, I peered towards the farm where my aunt lived, but could see no light. I tried to moisten my lips, but my tongue was swollen with thirst and my throat felt parched. I had to find someone to talk to — to give me food and water. Without thinking, I approached my aunt's farm at a run.

In moments, I was there, standing by the roadside, trying to pick out the path to the house, for it was overgrown with tangled grass and I could no longer see the fence and gate which at one time surrounded our yard. I gave up, and stumbled to the house, tearing the grass which caught at my feet.

The house was silent, dark and lonely as I neared the front door. But familiar odours reached me as I came closer, and they were comforting — there was the scent of rotting wood, washed with lye and beef-fat soap. This was Aunt Matilda — she smelled that way herself. Over to one side of the yard, I picked out the outline of the waterpump over the well — which again conjured childhood visions of an old man deep in thought. And the old laundry tub still hung grey against the dark, weather-beaten siding of the house.

I tried the door and found it locked. I knocked, gently at first, but there was no reply. I knocked again, louder, until my knuckles ached.

"Aunt Matilda? Are you in? It's me, Snit. I've come home. Let me in!"

Have you ever known a sleepless night — a night so silent you could hear the footsteps of a spider through it? I strained, and heard a sound, deep and far away in the house.

Then suddenly the door creaked open, and I smelled a sour, fevered face close to me.

"Snit! What do you want with me? Why did you come back? Get out! Go away and leave a poor woman in peace. I don't want to ever see you again — nobody wants to see you! Now go!" Her voice was so fierce it sounded like a burst of compressed air.

"Aunt Matilda — it's all right! I know you're all by yourself, and I won't bother ya none. I've just come visiting. Let me in — everything will be all right again!"

But she didn't move.

"Nothing will ever be right again, Snit. Never again! I can't hold you back with my hands. You've grown some. But you're not wanted here any more by me or the folks hereabouts." Her voice sounded tired and distant now. Then she walked back into the house, leaving the door open.

I hesitated a moment, then followed her in.

Only three years had gone by, but the face staring at me across the pine table in the light of the kerosene lamp had aged by ten times those three years. It was frightening — saddening. Her eyes were dead and tired, like those of a dog peering into a sudden bright light after coming in from the dark outdoors. Her hair, too, had turned a yellow-grey and hung over her shoulders and face in sticky strands. The brown-flecked skin of her face and neck was crinkled and dry, like a piece of ancient chamois cloth which had been rolled into a ball when wet and allowed to mildew. She wore a dark, nondescript outer coat, which showed signs of having been worked and slept in, and which had ragged ends on the sleeves and along the bottom. Yet she seemed in place in that kitchen, where the stove had food cooked onto it and the walls were soiled and cracked.

Aunt Matilda's hands trembled violently as she pushed a cup of tea across the table to me. They were such thin hands, and the sinews showed through the parched, fallen skin.

"Don't stare at me like that! I can still count to one hundred," she said, and grinned.

Her teeth were long, thin and badly decayed. Then, for no reason at all, her eyes lit up quickly, and I bent my head down. I was home, and things I had forgotten and learned not to fear began flooding my memory.

"I know you can, Aunt Matilda. Is the land in crop this summer?"

She glanced at me suspiciously and her tiny, tragicomic mouth set firmly. She lifted her cup to her lips without answering. But she was splashing her tea, her hands were trembling that violently now. I watched the hot liquid trickle down her wrist and underneath the ragged sleeve of her coat.

I had been taken away from my mother and my Aunt Matilda. At the "home" it was rumoured I had been taken because of insanity in my family. Yet when I asked Mrs. McGilvray any questions about it, she just stared at me and gave no reply. So I used to lie awake at nights, thinking — thinking about my father and the frogs. It didn't make much sense. And still it did — for when I tried hard to recall my father, and my home and the hills where I had lived, I would remember the frogs as well.

My father was afraid of frogs — he was afraid of many things. There was a slough of stagnant water on the boundary line with the farm north of us. In the spring and early summer frogs croaked all night through, and father sat up with the light on and his eyes wild with fear. He walked about the kitchen a lot on those nights, with his hands cupped over his ears and keeping us awake with his pacing and muttering. Not that it bothered me much, for I got used to this, just as I got used to going to bed on a hungry stomach.

He had been a quiet man, with a little sprig of brown moustache under his nose. Every Sunday morning, he trimmed his moustache with scissors, and if my aunt or mother saw him and laughed at his vanity, he would get so embarrassed as to leave the house and sit in the yard until they apologized and called him in.

He was so shy — so completely helpless. He always sat on the bench nearest the door in church. If he walked along the road and met a neighbour coming towards him, he would be the first to step out of the road, and with his head bent low in confusion, wait until the neighbour walked by. We always owed money to Tom Whittles at the store — everybody did. My father would not go near the store, for he felt Whittles would pick on him — which he did — and humiliate him. So my aunt did our buying, and infrequently, when she felt like going out, my mother.

There was the Hallowe'en night when all hell broke loose in the countryside. My aunt didn't allow me to go out, so I lay in bed and planned what I would do to her when I got big and strong enough. I'd starve her and beat her, that's what I'd do.

Outside, the kids were setting up a lot of noise, yelling "Monkey Mandolin! Monkey Mandolin — come out and play!"

This was me they were calling for, but inside the kitchen my father and mother were arguing. He was supposed to go to the barn to finish his chores with the cattle and horses, but he felt all the shouting was against him, and he was afraid of getting stoned or hit by a kid.

"You damned coward!" I heard my mother shout at him.

"Leave him alone, Nellie — you're as foolish as he is," my aunt said in a quiet voice, but mother kept right on.

"All right — I'll get the boy to protect you!"

"Snit!" she called. "Get up and take your father to the barn. He's scared of the dark!"

I got up and went into the kitchen, avoiding my aunt's eye. Then I took my father by the hand and led him outside. He was crying, or it sounded like it, for his head was down and I couldn't see his face. I walked to the barn with him, and the kids didn't do anything, for I was set to lace the dickens out of anyone who picked on my pa.

He wasn't a good farmer, but he kept us as well fed and dressed as the next man. But he was wasteful in a lot of ways. He had a horse he doted on — a bay stud which he fed all year round on oat and barley chop. Other folk only used these choice feeds when they worked their horses. In the winter, the animals had to fend for themselves by pawing away snow and eating what they could find beneath.

My father used to harness the bay to the stoneboat and go out into the field to load stones and haul them against the fence until the field was clear of rock for one season. Each year it was the same, for every summer you plowed up as many stones as you had picked off the land the year before. Sometimes I would run out to help him. If he didn't see me coming, I'd find him talking to the horse as he worked. He also talked to the horse as he dressed him down for the night in the barn. I got quite a kick out of standing outside the barn door in the moonlight, listening to him apologize to the horse for working him so hard, and promising him all sorts of pleasant things "soon" — when times got better.

"He's just a kid — a kid who grew a moustache," my aunt would say to my mother when they thought I wasn't listening.

"Oh, God!" my mother would sigh bitterly. "Why don't you take him, if you feel so soft for him?"

Aunt Matilda would laugh in a high, terrible way.

"It's too late, Nellie! You shoulda thought of that fifteen years ago!"

Without any warning, the bay stud got colic and died. My father buried him on the hillside where he had led him to die. When he returned to the house, he sat down at the kitchen window and stared and stared into the yard. I remember how he held his chin in his hand, his fingers reaching up and hooked over his lower lip until his teeth became dry and dull in his face. When Aunt Matilda came into the house and saw him, she scolded him for sitting around, and asked him to go with her into the garden and help out with hoeing potatoes.

He wouldn't move, even when night came.

A couple of days of this, and we were all pretty worried about him. Mother and my aunt tried everything, but he just sat there and stared into the yard.

"Leave him alone, Matilda," my mother said with a hard laugh. "Just wait until he wants to eat, and we'll see if he gets anything for behaving like that — trying to scare us!"

Saying that didn't help, for pa didn't seem to miss his meals. He wouldn't even look at the tea Aunt Matilda made and held under his nose.

Mother went to bed, where she remained, coughing and moaning all day. In the evening, she rose and approached father.

"If only mother was alive — she'd know how to deal with you!" she shouted, stamping her foot.

Father looked up, dropping his hand away from his chin. For the first time I could remember, his voice was strong, and he looked hard into the face of my mother.

"I been thinking, Nellie," he said. "We did something awful wrong. All the fires in hell won't burn it out of you or me. . . ."

I never heard him finish what he was saying. Mother closed her eyes tight and pressed her hands against the sides of her head. Then, quick as a cat, she let go and jumped at me. She grabbed me by the arm and jerked me to my feet and away from the table, which surprised me, with her being so sick and all. She steered me to the door and ordered me out.

Aunt Matilda followed and led me down the road towards the church. She put her arm over my shoulder as we walked, and in a soft voice which was as sad as it was gentle, told me not to listen to what folks said, because folks like us were given to doing peculiar things sometimes, and talking like people with the fever or drink in them. We walked a long way that evening, and I felt very close to my aunt. I took the hand she held over my shoulder, and squeezed it with both of mine.

When we came back, mother had gone to bed, and I was surprised to hear my pa whistling cheerfully. He was sitting in front of the kitchen stove now, oiling up the old rifle he used for scaring owls in the scrub. Then he put a shell in the gun, and holding it over his arm, walked to me and Aunt Matilda. He patted me on the head and went out.

"Where you going?" my aunt asked, almost in a whisper. But father was gone.

Like a person in a dream, my aunt moved to the kitchen table, where she sat down. Then she stared into the lamplight, her face twitching something awful. I spoke to her, but she didn't hear me, so I went to bed.

Mother and she went to look for him in the morning. They found him with his face in the frog pond. They kept me home when they buried him, so I never did see what he looked like with the back of his head blown off. . . .

I will never forget how it hurt to have my first tooth pulled. But the death of my father did not leave any disturbing pain with me. His life had given me no particular joy or sadness, and like the ghost he was, he neither took anything nor left anything with me.

"I'm only glad he came to his senses long enough to end it this way. Who would have taken care of him in a few more years?" mother said to Aunt Matilda over supper one evening. My aunt glanced at me, then opened her lips to say something. But I never heard her thoughts, for she nodded her head and remained silent.

Aunt Matilda worked the fields alone after this, for mother was not a woman of the land. She hated the soil — the hot, dry summers, and the cold, windy winters which kept folks around the kitchen stove for warmth months on end. The harder Aunt Matilda worked, the less she spoke. I never helped, for she didn't ask me, and I did not volunteer, choosing instead to spend my time drifting around the neighbourhood and waiting for the next day, in hopes it would bring some exciting, interesting change.

It was the summer following my father's death that mother confined herself to bed as an invalid, and I lost interest even in her.

Some four miles to the east of us was a ravine which cradled a stream during the spring, when water ran off the hills from winter snow. The life of the stream was short. Two weeks after break-up the land was dry, and with no run-off to replenish it, the water in the stream-bed disappeared. Across this ravine, on a flat, windy bit of land, stood an old log schoolhouse which had been put up by some Norwegian settlers long before my time. Years ago, the stories have it, these people gave up trying to make a living off the dead soil of the hills, and emigrated back to the land of their ancestors. But the school was kept open.

I went to this school for one year — just long enough to pick up the alphabet and a raging hatred of the longarmed teacher, Miss Bowen, who always picked her ears with a hairpin while contemplating my punishment for coming late each morning. Not that it was all my fault. I had never been brought up to tell time — one day didn't crowd another, so hours were insignificant. Besides, we didn't have a clock in our house.

I dropped out of school earlier than other children of our parts. Some of them went two years.

There was an inspector of schools who lived in town. Each fall, he drove out to our community, calling on each of the farms here. He argued and shouted at our folk to send the kids to school, or he'd make trouble. But our people were suspicious of him and said they wouldn't. In a very official way he would then write down the names of all who resisted learning, and then before he left he threatened he'd see what he could do about it. He always said that, and nobody paid him any mind until he came around the next year. My aunt and mother didn't argue; they just walked away from him. But others argued and told him why they wouldn't send us to learn.

"We don't raise kids for school here!" folks would shout at him.

"A kid don't need to learn t'read and write for to be able to grow potatoes and oats! Give a kid a bit of school, and he stops obeying his elders and betters. Next thing, they run off — an' who's gonna take care of us when we get old?"

Maybe the school inspector was impressed by this argument, for he never did make trouble among us.

If there was such a thing as a meeting-place for our folk, then I would say it was the church. Here everybody congregated on a Sunday, and there was much singing, shouting and "hallelujahs" — all sweaty and hot, with their hands threshing the backs of the benches in front, and the floor creaking under pounding feet. Reverend Nigel Crowe was the preacher in our church. He lived in town and came out to preach his sermon, often arriving a day earlier so he could stay over with Tom Whittles at the store. They were good friends — even resembled each other in appearance.

Reverend Crowe was as bald as a stone on top and heavy around the stomach. He had large, bushy grey brows that twitched and jumped when he got worked up during his sermon about any sort of sinning.

"Why were the children of Israel punished?" he would thunder, his brows bouncing.

"They was sinnin'!" A churchful of feet would slam and hands would clap together.

"Why are we punished with the vengeance of drought?"

"We is sinnin', *sinnin'*, SINNIN'!" The voice of the congregation rose in a chant, and fifty frightened, gleaming faces leaned forward and stared at Reverend Crowe.

Quite often, the reverend got so fired up with his own preaching, he'd step down from the pulpit and walk right among his congregation, asking the same questions and getting the same answers.

"Where does the Almighty send the sinners?"

"To hell!" the congregation would shout back, a quaver of fear in their collective voice.

"And what happens in hell?"

"We burn — we burn!" A moan now, and scarey enough to give a kid the creeps.

After the sermon and the singing, Reverend Crowe would walk with Tom Whittles over to the store. Many of the folks were still excited by the church service, and would follow, hoping somehow that the minister would say more to comfort or fever them up. Tom Whittles wanted folks to follow, for it meant he'd be able to sell stuff in the store. So he'd argue mildly with Reverend Crowe as they walked. And close at his heels the country folk followed, listening hard.

Tom Whittles was a religious man. He resembled the minister in his baldness and fatness, although he lacked Reverend Crowe's shaggy brows and his voice was thinner. But he kept a Bible on his store counter at all times, right next to the weigh scales. He'd finger the Bible as he poured peanuts to sell to kids, cheating like the devil by pouring the nuts on the furthest end of the scale tray to make more weight. I discovered this trick long before I knew how it was accomplished. On a balanced small see-saw I placed a half-pound tin of tobacco against a half pound of peanuts I got from Aunt Matilda. The tobacco easily overbalanced the peanuts. Tom Whittles sold a lot of peanuts in his store, and I often wondered why Reverend Crowe didn't mention this sort of cheating in a sermon. Maybe he didn't know about it.

Yet, as I have said, Whittles was a religious, industrious man. Besides running his store, he knew how to build chimneys in houses. So he had more money than anybody else, and being alone without a family, he lived and dressed better than even Reverend Crowe. But he had a streak of hard meanness in him. One incident has remained fresh in my memory, because somehow what happened has a bearing, I feel, on all the events which followed.

Shortly after Stanley Muller died, Aunt Matilda had a way of suddenly getting mad at everyone and everything about her. She'd flare up and sound off on things which didn't concern her, and it used to upset my mother if it happened in a public place. This day was a Sunday, and I recall how Aunt Matilda fidgeted and twisted in her seat in church during the sermon, her face hot and her eyes dark and bothered. Folks sitting on the other side of her turned and stared at her, for she made small sounds under her breath while everybody was trying to hear Reverend Crowe.

After the sermon, Reverend Crowe moved down through the church to the back door, where Tom Whittles stood waiting to shake his hand. Folks rose and crowded outside. As always, Tom Whittles and the minister began walking to the store, followed by the usual crowd of people from the congregation. Before we were even out the church gate, Whittles was questioning the minister on Scripture, and Reverend Crowe was replying in a firm, strong voice.

"What's he saying?" Aunt Matilda was crowding forward to be alongside the two men.

"What's got into you, Mat?" mother caught my aunt's arm and tried to hold her back.

"I just want to know what they're saying. I don't think either of them know what they're talking about!" my aunt said sharply. Mother looked at her hard.

"Be quiet and don't go making a fool of yourself!" she warned.

Aunt Matilda pressed on, however, and was among the first to get in when Whittles unlocked his store. By the time we came in, she was leaning on the counter, watching the storekeeper and Reverend Crowe, who were both behind the plank partition.

"I see what you mean, Reverend Nigel," Whittles was drawling, as he opened a bag of money to put into his change drawer. "Anyway, that was a right good sermon you gave this morning, and may the Lord hear it and take kindness upon us and you for it!"

"Thank you, brother Tom," Reverend Crowe replied, straightening his shoulders, for even though they spoke to each other by first names, the minister showed no intense warmth to the storekeeper while the store was full of people. He was still the preacher, just stepped down from his pulpit.

"Amen," someone in the back of the store echoed. One of the women asked about the price of lard at that moment.

Then, out of the blue, Aunt Matilda stopped all conversation.

"There is no God!" she exclaimed, her lips trembling and her eyes bright and sharp. Mother pushed in beside her and told her to mind what she was saying. Aunt Matilda pushed her away with an elbow.

Both Tom Whittles and Reverend Crowe turned with surprise. As for the rest of the crowd, you could hear a pin fall in that shop. The woman with the lard still held the package high over her head, and her arm froze there.

Whittles was the first to regain his senses. Looking over the heads of the folk in the store, he cleared his throat. Then he fixed a mean stare on my aunt.

"What did you say, you black-faced harlot?" he almost shouted, his voice high and thin. The preacher's brows began twitching with nervousness.

"There is no God!" Aunt Matilda spat out the blasphemy for the second time, and there were gasps of horror around us. But my aunt paid no mind. Looking straight in the eye of the storekeeper, she said in a dangerous voice, "You call me that name again, and I'll scratch your damned eyes out, Whittles!"

She looked like she could do it, too.

Whittles got scared then, and backed nearer to the minister. But at the same time the folk around us began to chide and scold Aunt Matilda; and when the noise picked up, mother got me and my aunt each by an arm, and steered us outside.

Mother did a powerful lot of coughing as we walked home that morning. She kept saying to Aunt Matilda that she had gone and fixed us all up proper with her big mouth and thoughtless ways. Then she said she knew what folks were thinking, and it was well enough to leave things as they stood.

At that point, Aunt Matilda stopped and turned to mother. As she spoke, she kicked road dust to one side with her foot.

"If there is a God, why don't He take pity on us and give us what the heart wants most? Why don't He give us some rain and a garden of flowers — just once? Why? Because there ain't no hell for us who live in this hell here — and as for the other place, it's all a nice story and nothing more!"

Which was talk way over my head, so I walked on by myself without listening to what mother had to say in reply. They argued all the way home.

Next Sunday, folks avoided us at church meeting, and whispered and pointed in our direction when they thought we weren't looking. For the first time in my life, I felt hot and choked up among all these people and all the secret things they thought. When Reverend Crowe started in singing and waving his hand to get everybody in the congregation singing with him, I said to mother I wanted a pee, and sneaked outside.

The church ground was small, and by the time I got out, there were about six other kids standing around trying to get some action going. They were pushing against one another, and one kid was grinding on the toes of a smaller guy with his heel, trying to get the kid to fight. When they saw me, they all made a circle around me like I was something strange and new.

"Fee! Fee! Fee! Yore aunt's a bad-un, and she ain't got no right staying around here in a chrishun community!" It was Mickey Rogers who said that. Mick was a kid who lived one farm north of us, and whom I could lick hands down any time. I started for him, and the circle broke and scattered. When they were at a safe distance, they all shouted like a bunch of magpies.

"Go home, ya little bugger, and take yer aunt with you, if ya know what's good fer her!"

"We'll get ya, Mandolin!"

Mick got out the gate and on the road, so I gave up chasing

him and started walking back into the church.

"Yah! Yah!" he shouted, with his dirty hands cupped over his mouth. "They'll take ya away to a little bastard home! Yuh'll see— They're makin' a paper on ya! Ya'll see! The Mandolins are bad-uns!"

"The Mandolins are buggers!" the other kids started to singsong, and I was glad to get back into church and over to my aunt and mother.

three

A few weeks after, one of our cows broke pasture. Before I brought the cow back and my aunt finished repairing the damaged rails, we were late for church. Mother was waiting in front of the house, and when my aunt signalled we were ready to go, she pouted and said she didn't know whether she should be seen arriving late in church.

"Don't argue — come on!" Aunt Matilda growled, and mother came without further complaint.

Reverend Crowe was already in his sermon when we entered the church. But when he saw us, he lowered his book and became silent. Mother became embarrassed and almost tripped over her feet as she hurried to be first in our seats, for all eyes in the congregation were on us now. I felt my aunt go tense and tight beside me. My own hands became sticky and cold, for I had never known this sort of interruption in a church meeting before. As we took our seats, I looked up and noticed the hands of Reverend Crowe were trembling, although he was standing very stiff and erect, and staring hard at Aunt Matilda. He cleared his throat, and the church congregation stirred with excitement.

"Matilda Mandolin — will you stand up and come before the congregation!" Reverend Crowe suddenly ordered, his shaggy brows a heavy straight set below his temples.

My aunt swallowed hard, but did not rise. I could feel the hot breath of the congregation as everyone leaned forward to close in on us.

"What for I come up?" Aunt Matilda asked in a thin voice.

"To beg forgiveness of the folks and God Almighty for your sinfulness and blasphemous ways."

"And supposin' I don't?"

A slow colour was rising to the preacher's cheeks. He was glancing around over his congregation, as if looking for someone to help him.

"I'm warning you, Matilda Mandolin," he said, but his voice wasn't as firm as he would have wanted it to be. "I'm warning you — I've discussed this matter with the church elders. You're being given a chance to clear yourself, and you had better do so right now. The Lord don't take no tomfooling with the likes of you!"

"Go kiss my ass, you Bible-thumping bastard!" Aunt Matilda said fervently. Rising to her feet, she upped and left the church, with everybody staring open-mouthed after her. Without thinking what I was doing, I rose and followed her, leaving mother behind. She was already in tears, and bent low in her seat to hide herself. I didn't want to watch my mother cry, any more than I wanted to stay cooped in the church, waiting for folks and Reverend Crowe to start burning over what my aunt had done.

Aunt Matilda ran all the way home. I called to her to wait as I ran after her, but she didn't hear me. When I got in the house after her, she'd closed herself in the bedroom and locked the door. I heard her sobbing.

When mother came home, she looked pale and tired. She had a red welt across one cheek, where someone had hit her with something sharp. From this day on, the differences between my mother and my aunt became as marked and strong as the changes of night and day. Aunt Matilda became fighting angry, staying away from the house and involving herself in hard work around the farm. My mother sort of gave up trying for anything any more. She got thinner and less anxious to rise from bed in the mornings. My aunt and she seldom spoke after this, except to argue or complain. At first I was worried about mother, when she wouldn't get up some days at all, not even to eat. Aunt Matilda didn't seem anxious about her, and soon I forgot to worry, for it seemed like things had always been this way with us.

There are so many answers I want to find to many questions which no one ever explained to me. Maybe folks in these parts have it in them to be suspicious of two husbandless women living together. Or maybe they never liked us — just let on they did in other times. We used to have neighbours who called in once in a while to chew stories with my aunt and mother. Then, there was nobody calling at all. I found more and more folks chasing me off when I went calling on kids to play with. The only people who paid any notice to us at all were odd drunks driving home in wagons from town late at night. They would stop on the road by our gate and yell across the yard to my aunt, asking if she was lonely enough to let a good man in. Whenever this happened, Aunt Matilda would come tearing out of her bed and out into the yard, shaking her fist and threatening damnation on the drunks if they didn't leave her alone and go their way. The drunks would laugh like whinnying stallions, and then with wagons clattering they would drive away.

Across the road from us, but with their buildings on the other side of the hill and out of view from our yard, lived the Shnitkas. They had a whole bunch of kids, with one boy my age. His name was Harry, and he was smaller than me because he had rickets as a baby. He used to collect feathers, which he kept in a tobacco can. I saw him prowling around our field one day, searching for magpie feathers. Since he would no longer play with me, I ran over to torment him. He was a funny kid, with a nose always running; and when he spoke, his words came out muffled as if his tongue was tied to the roof of his mouth.

"What you got there?" I shouted, as I bore down on him.

With no trouble at all, I took the feathers he had gathered away from him.

As I said, he was smaller, but he tightened his fists and came at me. I grabbed him and threw him over on his side. He got up, crying with anger and hurt.

"We'll fix ya! We'll fix that witch of an aunt of your'n and yore muvver, too — we'll fix ya good. We'll fix ya special!" he shouted at me, and then ran away.

We didn't go to church any more, so even our Sundays had nothing exciting happening. Mother stayed in bed, waiting for death. Aunt Matilda spent long days working in the fields and garden. They didn't ask me to help, and I didn't. One day was like another to me, and they were all boring and depressing. I walked around the yard kicking stones back and forth. Some folks drove by on the road during a day, but none of them waved to me, so I couldn't be bothered even waving to them.

Then there was the day old man Shnitka came over, his face hot and dirty, and his eyes bothered by something terrible.

"Where's yore mother?" he asked.

I pointed over my shoulder to the house. He began walking in the direction I pointed.

"She's sick in bed," I said after him. He stopped and shuffled his feet in the dirt uncertainly.

"Where's yore aunt, then?"

Without replying, I ran out into the field to get Aunt Matilda. When we returned, Shnitka was still standing in the yard, in the same place I had left him.

"Well?" Aunt Matilda brushed her hair back, and looked at our neighbour suspiciously.

"I come to tell ya," Shnitka faltered, his gaze fixed halfway up my aunt's stomach, because he was a shy man and could look no one directly in the face. "There's a paper making the rounds in these parts. I didn't sign it, Matilda, because I don't go for this sort of thing at all. So I come to tell ya, before it's too late."

"What ya talking about?"

Shnitka looked at me, then at my aunt. Then he turned away from us and stood facing the fields to the north.

"They is signing a petition to take the young-un away from here!" he blurted, pointing a thumb in my direction. "Paper says you and his mother are not quite all there in the head, and the boy's gonna grow up like that and be bad. Don't say to anybody I came atelling ya — I don't want no trouble with my neighbours."

Without another word, Shnitka walked away, crossing the road to his own farm. My aunt stood there with her mouth open. Looking up at her, I saw that the colour had left her cheeks, showing great blotches of tan on her thin face.

"What's it mean, what he said?" I asked.

"Nothin' — just talk. Folks have to have some talk, that's all. You go in, or this sun will melt your brains," she said, pushing me towards the house.

Soon after, there came an afternoon so hot and sticky that even Aunt Matilda stayed home in the shade.

"Let the place go to pot — I'm not aimin' to roast alive!" she said. This had been the day she was to go out in the fields and pinch off thistle blossoms to prevent the weeds from going to seed. She and I were sitting around the front door, watching flies drowsily examining the door-frame. We both saw the car, which bumped its way along the road and came to a stop at our gate.

"Look!" Aunt Matilda exclaimed, then shouted over her shoulder, "We got company, Nellie — in a car!"

Only the school inspector and the police drove a car in those days, so we were pretty excited. Mother came out of bed, and the first thing she did was comb her hair for the occasion.

Both doors of the car came open at the same time. Out of one stepped a mountie with yellow-striped blue breeches and a tunic red as fire. It was too hot for a hat, so he didn't wear one. Out of the other door appeared a tall, grey-haired man wearing a brown suit. He carried a large briefcase under his arm. They stopped momentarily, glanced at our house, and approached.

As I said, our door was open for coolness, and these two men came right in without knocking. Aunt Matilda rose to put on water for tea, and mother quickly sat in the chair she had vacated to be nearest the door and the men.

"Howdy. I'm Corporal Kane, and this is Mr. Webber," said the policeman, grinning quickly at nobody in particular.

Mr. Webber stood in the doorway. There was a long silence, for they didn't ask any questions or state the purpose of their visit. Instead, they searched our house — not searching by walking around and turning things over, but snoop-searching, examining the floors and walls, and craning their necks to see into the bedrooms. They both looked up to see into the cupboard when Aunt Matilda opened it to get the tea. I was watching them, and getting sore, for I never have liked snoops.

After they had seen into everything possible to see from where they stood, Corporal Kane looked down at mother and grinned a friendly smile.

"I'm sorry, but which one of you ladies is Mrs. Mandolin?" he asked.

"She is!" Aunt Matilda snapped without turning from where she stood at the stove. "You're not paying no friendly visit, so whatever's on your minds, get on with it!"

Corporal Kane coughed to clear his throat, and his face turned red. My aunt's rudeness left him with nothing to say, and he turned to his companion, pointing to my mother at the same moment, as if to say, "Do something — here she is!"

Mr. Webber stepped into the room now.

"Mrs. Mandolin, we'd like to have a word with you — privately."

He looked at me, and then at Aunt Matilda. I rose to my feet, but Aunt Matilda didn't even turn, and I could see they weren't going to push her none. I didn't want to miss a word of what the mountie and Webber had to say, so instead of waiting for mother to order me outside, I crossed the kitchen into my bedroom. I closed the door behind me, then pressed my ear against it to listen.

First thing, I heard them ask Aunt Matilda to leave the the room. Quick as a whip, she replied with a dirty suggestion about where *they* could go if they wanted to.

The voices of Corporal Kane and the other man were no longer polite now.

"Mr. Webber is from the Provincial Welfare Department, and we didn't drive all this way to listen to nonsense. Just remember that!" Kane raised his voice.

"Please, Matilda — don't get us in trouble with these folks," my mother begged.

After this the questions began, hot and fast. How much was my mother earning from the farm, and how much were we spending on food and clothes? Why wasn't I made to go to school? And were we in the habit of making trouble in the community? Did we go to church without missing a Sunday — and who was parson in our church? What happened to my father? Were my grandparents normal, or had they been to a hosiptal for observation? Had anybody still living been to a hospital? After the first few questions, mother began to cry.

Aunt Matilda took over the answers. Of course grandpa and grandma had never seen the inside of a hospital! A tree had fallen on the old man, and grandma died in bed of old age — and would they get the hell out and mind their own business instead of bothering folks who were busy.

Mr. Webber had a voice about as sympathetic as a rusty hinge. "We're just doing our job, madam. You understand we have to — a petition was sent to our department about —"

"A petition? You know where you can stuff your goddam petition!" Aunt Matilda was really going on.

Suddenly, my door was yanked open by the policeman, and I was pressed so tightly against it listening that I went sprawling into the kitchen. The cop took hold of my collar and lifted me to my feet.

"Let's go, Roy," he said to the welfare man, still holding me. "I've got the kid, so let's beat it. This broad is driving me buggy."

With a shove, he pushed me outside the door, and began steering me for the car. I fought like a cat, and almost broke

43

free of the corporal. But Webber closed in and caught me by the other arm. Against the two of them, I could only bite and kick, but I couldn't hold back. When they held me at the car, and Webber reached to open the door, I looked back at our house. Through the open kitchen door I saw my mother sitting at the table, her head buried in her hands. But my aunt was right behind me, her eyes wild as she bashed Corporal Kane this way and that about the face with her hard little fists. She had already given him a pretty mean scratch over his left eye.

"Uniformed punk!" she shouted at the mountie. He was mad by now, and letting go of me with one hand, he hit my aunt with his fist across the mouth. She fell down by the car, both her hands clutching at her lips, and blood oozing out between her fingers.

The two men threw me into the car, and drove off quickly, with the car heaving and tossing over the bumpy road.

The lamp sputtered. Home. Slowly, my good Aunt Matilda was getting over the shock of seeing me back. A little smile came to her lips. She reached out with the pot and poured me another cup of tea.

"Did they hurt you bad, boy?" she asked, as if sifting my memories with me.

"No — not where it shows or matters particularly," I replied, and wondered if she had a bed for me to sleep the night. The door to what had been my room was open, but it was pressed against the floor with the sag of the house. Yet I hoped that inside, the room might have been preserved — that something of me had not been forgotten and neglected.

I woke during the night and sat up, thinking it was time to get up and get ready to open the coffee-shop. As I moved, the noisy bedsprings creaked fit to wake the dead, and I heard Aunt Matilda groan in the next room. I became alert and aware of my surroundings, and it gave me a great feeling of sadness.

There was silence now, except for the faint rustle of the settling house. My room was in darkness, and smelled of vegetables and dust. Only a pencil of moonlight showed through a chink in the wall. I reached for it, and playing it on the palm of my hand, imagined I could feel it tickle me.

There had been only one stop when they drove me away — at Elsie's in town, where they bought me a sandwich of stale bread and leathery chicken, which I could taste even now. Then out of town on the black tar highway to Edmonton and the orphanage.

They didn't call it an orphanage, they called it a welfare home — The Merciful Redeemer Welfare Home; but after a while I found I was the only one who had a living parent. The place was run by Mrs. McGilvray, a fat, crosseyed woman who looked like a tired cook.

Across the road and three blocks to the east was the school in which we were to get our learning. In it there was a reminder of the home. Aged and water-soiled plaques saying "God Bless Our Home" hung on the walls of both buildings. I later learned that they had been embroidered and framed by a Polish kid who became a sailor. But that was a long time ago.

After school, we were to come directly to the home. We were then to repay the generosity shown to us, and also build our characters, by growing potatoes on a twenty-acre field which surrounded the main buildings. Those of us who did not want field work were given the alternative of staying indoors and scrubbing miles of floors in corridors and dormitories. This work was done by hand in a kneeling position, and I didn't know of a boy who could take it more than three evenings in a row without limping badly with bruised knees.

"You are now among nice, Christian boys, like yourself. Stay out of trouble, and you will be happy here. Supper will be at six o'clock," Mrs. McGilvray had said to me even before I was through the gate, where she met me.

"One other thing," she added, as I followed her to the dormitory. "We do not allow our boys to talk about where they came from. We just want them to be happy."

She turned then, and with her one good eye on my face, took me in a half-hearted hug. Her clothes smelled of turnip and sweat.

The boys didn't talk about their pasts — but not because Mrs. McGilvray had ordered them not to. Most of them had been in the home so long they just didn't remember anything so far back. Lying in bed when the lights were out at night, I would tell the boys who shared the big dormitory with me about the hills, and about my aunt and mother — even about Johnny Swift and the Shnitka kid across the road. The boys listened, asked questions in whispers, and never told on me.

For the first few days, I was shown around the buildings, and made to clean up the kitchen and our sleeping-room. Then came the time to decide whether I would take duties indoors, or out in the fields. Dave, an older boy who shared the room we slept in, advised me to ask for field duties. He was a tall, thin, blond-haired fellow with a sad face. I liked him right off the start, because he never spoke rough to anyone, and always stopped to help the smaller kids when they were behind in a job. Mostly because Dave worked in the fields himself, I asked for field work.

It was a smart thing to do, for here we got the benefit of fresh air and sunshine. Nobody worked very hard, for we were supervised by a Mr. Swanson, an elderly man who had something wrong with his back and could not walk around much. I soon learned to work away from where he sat or leaned on his cane watching us, and to go where the others were digging and spading. Here we could talk, and work slower.

Once one of the boys leaned on his spade and began picking his nose.

"Here," Dave said angrily to the kid, "don't stand there doing nothing, or we'll get Mr. Swanson in trouble, and they'll get someone really tough to supervise us. Don't take advantage of a man that's easy — there ain't that many of them around."

Dave never talked about himself, so I knew no more about

him than what he did and the few things he said, yet I remember him so well even now, and feel proud of having had him as a friend once. If only he had done what I later did — together, the two of us would have done great things.

We were made to pray before supper, and any of the boys caught mumbling their prayers instead of showing genuine devotion were deprived of their pudding after the meal. So we learned to pray loudly and with zeal.

A few weeks after I was in the home, I felt restless, hot and closed in. At the risk of waking the others in my room, I rose, and putting on my clothes went downstairs through the dining-hall and outside. It was cool outside, with a light wind blowing from the south. I thought first of just walking around the garden, but there was a chance Mrs. McGilvray might still be up and see me, so I scaled the fence around the grounds, and was out on the road. I knew I was breaking a strict house regulation, but figured I could make it to the highway junction and back without being missed.

I was nearing the intersection where our street met the main highway, when a gasoline truck came roaring around the right-of-way circle. He was coming too fast, and halfway around the circle one of his rear wheels hit the outside curb of the concrete ring which bordered the island. The truck lurched and swayed, but continued driving on. The safety hatch on its tank trailer snapped open with a pop I could hear, and a sheet of gasoline sprayed the street. The truck driver hadn't noticed, for in a minute he was gone down the right-of-way into the city.

I could smell the gasoline now, and hurried forward in the darkness. However, before I reached the intersection, a car came in the same direction the tanker had taken. As the car passed over the wet street, one of its passengers must have tossed a lit cigarette out of the window, for no sooner had the vehicle cleared the intersection than the street burst into flame with a dull *whoosh*. I was fascinated by the heat and light the burning gasoline made, and was hardly aware of cars drawing up from all directions — the shouting and hurrying of people in a panic.

"Pull the fire-box — hurry!" someone shouted from a distance, and someone near me shouted back, "Where is the alarm box?"

One of the people in that crowd must have known the location of the box, because a fire truck soon appeared, with lights flashing and siren slowly wailing into silence. The darkly caped firemen played a hose on the street, covering the burning gasoline with a milky foam. It was all over with, and I was just about to leave, when a firm hand gripped my shoulder and turned me around.

It was the fat cook of a house-mother at the welfare home, Mrs. McGilvray.

"What are you doing out here?" she hissed through her teeth, and her left eye looked hard into mine. I opened my mouth to explain, but couldn't get the words out.

She pressed my shoulder hard now, and I nearly shouted with the pain. Then she led me down the road back to the home. When we reached the grounds, she unlocked the gate and motioned me through. I waited for her as she locked up. When she pocketed the key, she stepped in front of me, and very casually, as if it were part of the locking-up procedure, she struck me across the face with the back of her hand.

My eyes felt as if they would fly out of my head, and I felt dizzy and sick to the stomach.

"You pig! You big, dirty, overfed, ugly old pig!" I screamed at her when I felt steadier on my feet.

She struck me again, this time a double-handed blow over the head, and I fell to my knees. She sure knew where and how to hit. Try as I would to cover my head with my hands, she always found an unprotected part of my cheeks or temples at which to slap and punch. I was dazed with pain, and my nose ran as if my head had sprung a leak. I took my hands off my head and reached for her leg. Getting a firm hold, I sank my teeth deep into her ankle. I thought I heard her shout, but I'm not sure, for everything began spinning, and I fainted.

I was not allowed to school the following morning or for three mornings after, as my face was cut and swollen. But she woke me with the others all the same. I was taken off field work and ordered to clean the hallways leading to the central washrooms. I scrubbed, but when the day ended I could not eat, for even walking made me ill to the stomach.

As I scrubbed and rescrubbed the same floors day after day, I plotted my escape for the time when I felt strong enough to do so.

My opportunity came on the fourth night following my beating. It was easy. Our sleeping quarters were on the second floor of the building, directly over the dining-hall. Mrs. McGilvray had her apartment behind the dining-hall, alongside the kitchen, and facing into the field, away from the road. From her apartment, Mrs. McGilvray put out our lights at nine o'clock on days preceding school, and at ten on Friday and Saturday nights. As this was a Thursday, the lights went out early, but I lay wide awake, listening to the whispers of the boys in my room.

I had wanted to tell Dave of my plans, to urge him to go with me. But I was afraid he might betray my intentions. Yet there had been moments during the evening when I felt he must know. After supper, he had wandered away in the direction of the north porch, which had been rebuilt into a small, cold library. I went after him, but in the reading-room a group of boys had gathered, and there was no privacy.

Now it was night, and the lights had gone out. I lay in the dark, listening, and trembling with fear.

"Quiet, you guys, I wanna sleep." I tried to make my voice sound weary. Soon the whispers died, and there was such a silence I could hear the roar of traffic on the distant highway.

I was able to count the sleepers in my room — almost tell them apart by the sleep sounds they made. I thought perhaps Dave might be awake, suspecting I was leaving.

"Dave." I formed the word with my lips, but could not bring myself to say it.

I waited for about a half hour to make certain they were asleep before I stirred. Then I got out of bed and dressed very quietly. Taking my shoes in my hand, I tiptoed to the window and pushed it up. It made a scraping sound and I flattened against the curtain. Two beds down, someone mumbled and turned. Afraid I was detected, I quickly climbed over the sill of the window and jumped out, landing in the soft garden earth outside. The dining-room window opened on the garden, and glancing inside I saw the light under the door of Mrs. McGilvray's apartment. There was no time to waste, so I went across that garden at a gallop. Only after I had scaled the fence did I stop long enough to get my shoes on and laced tightly.

And after that I ran — faster and longer than I had ever run before. I ran through back lanes, blindly and in a panic of fear — going to no particular place, just running away from the last one as fast as I could. I ran over peoples' lawns and between houses. Fortunately, I met no one in my flight, or the entire city would have been alarmed by me.

And as I ran, I cursed. I cursed the fat cook of a housemother. I cursed my aunt and my mother, and Tom Whittles, and the preacher, and the underhanded pig of a cop, Corporal Kane. I cursed the grey-haired man in a brown suit who didn't like dirty kids. One day! One day I would look them up, and then they would know what it was like to be taken from the hills and brought to a welfare home where they beat you and made you work like a slave!

There was no end to the city. Like one huge cement ant-hill, it stretched forever. And yet, I ran out of it — out of the lawns and row houses, the lonely street lights that looked down at me like filthy old men, the rickety warehouses with bottled-up anger in their small windows. I was on the highway, running from the last street lamp, with only the long white lines showing on the hard road before me. Still running, I pointed my finger and shouted at each white marker on the road. My chest was burning and my lips cracked with thirst.

I stopped and sat down on the pavement to rest. I could go no further this way. My head wobbled, and my shoulders pressed hard on my body. Loosening my shoes, I wiped my forehead with the sleeve of my shirt.

Behind me, the glow of the city rose into the sky, yet I had lost any distinct, individual light. I then turned to look down the highway into the countryside. Some distance away, I thought I could see a faint light twinkling. Feeling terribly thirsty now, I got up and walked towards this light.

four

I walked past the strong-smelling gasoline pumps and pushed open the door of the brightly lit coffee-bar. The man was turned away from me when I entered. He was wiping glasses and arranging them on a shelf. One of those bony, thin people he was, with a shirt that hung loose off his sharp shoulders. His pants were buckled tight and crinkled all around him as if they were pulled in by a drawstring. I sat down on a stool at the counter and waited.

He turned a long, hungry face to me and his eyes widened. They were soft eyes, almost like those of a woman, and blue in colour. I noticed with surprise how out of place his heavy lips were in that sharp, dry face.

"Yessirree, son?" he spoke, but I only stared at him stupidly. I thought he smiled ever so little, and then he walked away and filled a glass with coke and ice.

"You been hit by a car, son?" he asked, when he placed the fizzing glass in front of me.

I shook my head, for my throat was dry and hot and I couldn't make a sound. He returned to his work, and I drank the Coke greedily. When I finished, I felt cool and good again.

"Thanks!" I said. "Thanks a lot!"

He continued with his work. Only when he had put away the last glass did he turn again and walk toward where I sat. He wiped his hands slowly, looking me up and down carefully as he did so.

"Now, where you going and why?" he asked in a firm voice. "You'd better tell me all about it before I call an ambulance and the cops, or just take it in my mind to kick the shit out of you for trying to pull a fast one on me."

I told him the story, but only from the time I was brought to the orphanage. I didn't feel he needed to know about the hills where I was raised, or about Aunt Matilda and my mother and pa. Even if he had wanted to know, I couldn't explain to him, for I no longer knew the truth of what I had seen and lived through. But he didn't ask. After I finished my story, he lit a cigarette and looked at me a long time. Yet he wasn't examining me any more — he knew I had not lied when I spoke. He was just thinking.

"How old are you?" he asked, after a few minutes so silent I could hear the buzz of the tube lights in the ceiling.

"Fourteen."

"Kinda big for your age, ain't you?"

"My ma used to say I growed like a weed."

"What's your name?"

"Snit Mandolin."

"Snit — that's a nice name — different, too. Mine's Pete — Pete Olson." He leaned forward towards me, and his clear, woman's eyes were excited.

"Listen carefully, Snit. They'll be looking high and low for you, because they're responsible. But" — his face broke into a broad, crinkly smile — "I ain't one to help keep an animal or a kid caged against its wish. I can't do much for you, but if you want to stay with me here and help out, you're welcome to. I can't pay you wages 'cause the place don't bring that much in, but you'll get food and clothing, and if business is good, there'll be a little extra. Also learn a trade for the time you're old enough to step out on your own. Means a lot, that. But mind, you're not to talk to anyone about yourself, or I'll have my neck in a noose good. Just say I'm your uncle or something, if anyone asks you. But best you don't talk at all."

Pete had two gasoline pumps in front of his place, and a garage for minor repairs and servicing. Back of the garage, adjoining the kitchen, was a little room in which he kept small auto parts and dry confectionery. I slept on the floor of this room the first night. The next day, Pete brought me a cot and bedding. I helped him move the other stuff out and get the room cleaned for my own.

Working for Pete was hard, and the hours were long. He had a home in the city, so I was left alone when the garage and coffee-bar were closed for the night. He was his own boss, yet he seldom closed before midnight, and was open before eight in the morning. But I enjoyed working for him. He taught me how to operate the pumps and count change on gasoline and oil sales. Then he taught me to change tires and do quick tune-ups on a sluggish carburetor, as well as oil changes and lube jobs. I worked hard and learned quickly. Before winter came, Pete seldom had to go outside to help me.

One afternoon things were slow for a few minutes, and I joined Pete in the bar for a coffee. A big car came on the tarmac, but it stopped short of the pumps, so I waited for the driver to come in. He was one of those guys who can always find ways of giving you trouble — a fat, red-faced, round-bellied guy with mean eyes and a soggy cigar stuck between his teeth. That's the type who breathe down your neck when you're trying to work, and who always pretend to know the other fellow's job inside out.

"Ya got a mechanic on duty?" he asked loudly as he came through the door. "I got a wobble in my front end, and I wanna adjustment."

Before I could catch myself, I turned and took a fast look at his gut-bag. I couldn't choke back a grin, so I stuck my face back into my coffee mug. Pete saw the look on my face, because he coughed hard before he could reply.

"Mr. Snit will see to your car." Pete nodded in my direction and winked.

"That kid! G'wan — I wanna mechanic — some joe who knows one end of a car from the other!"

"Mr. Snit is a very capable mechanic," Pete's voice became pretty hard. I looked up, and saw that his face had set like he was sporting for a fight. Fat Boy backed down.

"Aw, awright. But he better do a good job."

I didn't mind the fat bugger breathing down my neck as I jacked up the car and started in on aligning his wheels. I worked fast, but carefully, for I wanted Pete to be proud at having trusted me. When I finished and brought the car down, Fat Boy grunted and took it for a run up and down the tarmac. He stopped on the far side, on the highway entrance, and called me over.

"Say, kid — you're all right! Works like a charm! Say — that guy sure stuck by you when I got salty. What's he like — y'know — sweet on ya? Ya can tell me, I got an open mind. He is a queer, ain't he?"

I didn't know what the hell he was talking about, but I didn't like the oily smile he was giving me. I didn't know what to say, so I just stood there looking at him. He got pretty uncomfortable, and his face became redder.

"Awright, so it's none of my business. Here — betcha he don't pay you much. Here! This is for you — don't tell him I gave it to ya!" He pulled out a wad of money from his pocket, and peeling off a five-dollar bill, stuck it out to me. Then he went into the coffee-bar to pay the repair charge to Pete.

I didn't tell Pete about the tip, and it sort of bothered me. I put the money in a cigar-box which I kept under my bed, along with other tips I got from folks from time to time during the three years I stayed and worked with Pete. But if Pete knew, he never let on, for which I was grateful; but it still bothers me not telling him.

Pete was good on getting me things. Once a month, he used to bring me a new shirt or sweater, or a new pair of slacks. I took good care of these clothes, and wore the garage coveralls almost all the time. A few times he bought me books, but as he never read himself, he wasn't much on these. The ones he gave me were baby books, with pictures and big type you could read a block away. At Christmas time, when calendars came from his suppliers, he used to tack them up himself in my room, and it gave a lot of colour. Almost felt like my room had been repainted.

We didn't talk much, for most days we were apart and busy, and at nights I wanted to get to bed first off. Mornings, I got up before he came in, and I would light the fires under the coffee urns for him, as well as grease and heat the hotcake iron. A fleet of trucks coming in from Saskatoon would pull in between eight and nine each morning, and the drivers would come in for breakfast. Pete had his hands full getting the breakfasts prepared before the men arrived, so I ran the pumps and service garage on my own in the mornings.

Pete appreciated my getting things set up for him in the coffee-shop. Each morning he'd wag his head with surprise and smile at me as he took his coat off and put on his white apron.

"Snit, you're quite a boy for get-up-and-go in the morning! Tell you what — one of these nights we're gonna lock up early and go on the town — just you and me."

And he lived up to his promise — about a year after I was with him. We closed up at six and I changed into my neat new clothes. Then we drove into town to see a picture called *How Green Was My Valley*. The thought of going into town no longer frightened me. We even drove past the welfare home, and I pressed my face against the car window to see into the fields. A group of boys were burning leaves, and I saw Mr. Swanson among them, leaning on his stick and watching. But the boys were too far away and I couldn't tell if they were new ones, or the fellows I had known. Then we were in the heart of the city, and Pete parked his car across the street from the theatre.

I ate three boxes of popcorn during the picture, and felt thirsty and sad. Pete just lay back in his seat and slept right through the movie. When I had seen the cartoon and news for the second time, I woke him, and we went to the coffee-bar in the theatre lounge, and Pete treated me to a strawberry milkshake.

"Good picture, wasn't it, Snit? Sure beats me how they can think up all them stories — and then you see them like that and could swear you was there and lived it all." He yawned.

"Yep," I said, and drank my milkshake. I was sort of hoping he might take me to his home so I could see what it was like. But he didn't. After I finished my drink, he drove me back to the garage and we never went out again.

Then came the third summer — hot and windy. Business was lighter than usual, and when our mail came, I watched Pete gloomily study his many bills, then toss them into a box behind the coffee counter.

"Jesus Christ! If a war don't come soon, the whole country's going to go bust!" he'd growl as he poured us a coffee each. Few cars stopped at the pumps any more, which made me wonder — where in hell do people buy their gas and oil when times get bad? The same number of cars were still passing by on the highway, yet our business was down. I asked Pete about it.

"Credit," he said. "The big guys can afford to give credit. You know — 'Fill 'er up now, and pay me next month.' Me, I can't give no credit even to myself."

Pete was a funny sort of guy when he got to talking. The way he figured it, a war would fix everything just right.

"Ya ever been in a war, Pete?" I asked, as I swallowed from the steaming coffee-cup, and then wished I hadn't, for it was like a furnace outside and the coffee burned all the way down my throat. Pete looked at me surprised-like.

"Me? In a war? Are you kidding? I couldn't fight my way out of a wet paper bag!"

"Then what for you want a war?"

"I dunno. It always seems to straighten things out. I dunno how these things work — it's the Jews that run the world — they got it all figured, and they work it just right for themselves. It's guys like you and me that's got to suffer."

"Ya ever known a Jew?" I asked on my second swallow.

"Naw — I never met a Jew in my life. Why did you ask that for?"

When the wind and heat got bad, a lot of dirt and dry weeds got blown on the tarmac around the pumps. I used to sweep up at first, but it didn't do any good, for the wind just carried the muck back as soon as I finished. Hosing the place down with water would have helped, but Pete didn't want the expense of pumping any more water than he had to have for the coffee-bar, So when the weather got really hot, I used to go into my room and lie down to get away from the sun and dust.

I was lying stretched out on my bed one afternoon, rubbing the toes of my moist socks back and forth across the bedrail and thinking of nothing at all. Pete had been coming and going without a word to me lately. He'd show up for a few hours in the morning. Then the telephone would ring and he'd answer it. Just like that, off would come his apron and on with his tweed sports coat.

"Keep the homestead together, Snit! I got some business in town!" he'd shout over his shoulder as he ran for his car. He'd gone off that way this morning.

So I lay in bed, thinking of nothing at all when I heard Pete clear his throat, and I looked up to see him standing in my doorway. His long face was wet with sweat. He was worried and uncomfortable, and kept his eyes down on his feet.

"Snit," he said, and bent down to brush some lint off his pants, "I guess I better tell you now as tomorrow. I sold the business.

I didn't understand what he said for a moment and just grinned back at him. Then it hit me.

"What ya mean? Ya mean you and I aren't gonna be here no more?" I said, jumping to my feet.

Pete really got bothered, and turned away from me as if to go out.

"Yep," he said over his shoulder. "I'm thinking of moving on to the coast and buy a little store some place. Hours are too long and lonely here, and I'm not a young man anymore.

You'll do all right, Snit. You're bright and handy with your hands. Betcha anything you'll get another job like nothing at all."

"But Pete! I wanna go with you — can't I?" I was scared clean through.

He didn't say anything, but I could tell by the way he hung his head and rested himself with one arm against the door-frame that he didn't want me any more.

"When I gotta go?" I asked.

"Any time you like."

He turned towards me, and it sort of shook me to see the tears in his eyes.

"I got something here for you, Snit — not much, but it's all I can afford, and it'll help you."

He fumbled in his shirt pocket and brought out an envelope, which he handed me. Without thinking on what I was doing, I opened it right there and then. Inside was a cheque for three hundred dollars.

I didn't even thank Pete. I didn't remember to. With everything in my life suddenly turned inside out, I had no way or desire of telling or showing Pete what I thought. It was no good my hanging around watching him close the station down, so that same day I got my things together and packed for him to ship out.[

"Where you planning to go?" he asked me over breakfast the next morning. I was dressed in a white shirt and my pants were nicely pressed. I had laid them out under my mattress and slept over them during the night to take the wrinkles out.

"Think I'll head out for the old home place."

"What? Into the hills?"

I nodded.

"You're stupid!" Pete was staring hard at me. "What you gonna do in that hell-forsaken place? I hear you can't even grow potatoes there!"

"That's a lie!" I argued. "We used to grow lots of potatoes — and barley so tall I used to get lost in it as a kid"

"Big deal!" Pete laughed. "I can drive you around to a few garages I know, and we'll find you a job for wages in no time at all. Put in eight or nine hours a day, and you're your own boss with money in the pocket and no worries in the world. Come on — finish your grub and we'll take a drive."

I was going back to the hills or nowhere at all, and I told Pete so. He rose from his stool, threw his arms apart, and blew a long whistle of air through his lips.

"Suit yourself — you're a man now," he said. Then he loaded what things I could carry into his car, and drove me through the city. When we reached the highway leading to my home town, I told him this would be far enough, and he stopped the car.

"Good luck, Pete!" was all I could say to him.

"I'll ship the rest of your things by bus. See ya!" He turned in the middle of the highway and drove back into town.

About an hour later, I hitched a lift with a gravel truck which was going right through to my town. By this time the wind had come up, hot and dusty. I slept much of the way, one of those neck-sore sleeps with my head thrown back over the dirty shoulder-rest of the seat. It was a ride on clanging tools and with crushing bumps, but I didn't mind, for I was going home and I was tired.

When we reached town, my head ached from the heat and my throat burned with thirst. Across the street, swinging in the wind, was the faded board sign, "Elsie's Coffee Shop & Eats."

I had arrived.

Aunt Matilda was suspicious as hell of me.

"How long you figuring on staying?" she demanded over breakfast. "And why did you come back?"

I didn't really know, so I said nothing and kept eating with my face pretty close to the table. She left her chair and rummaged about in an old coffee tin which stood on a shelf above the stove. She came back with a soiled piece of paper, which she unfolded as she sat down.

I had been watching her all morning, with shock and fear,

for in the light of day her appearance upset me as much as it had when I first saw her last night. What little flesh was left in her face had knotted and dried into short cords, as if she had been roasted by some fire, put out into the sun to dry, and then roasted again, until every drop of moisture in her body was evaporated.

This wasn't my Aunt Matilda — I never met this woman before. She wasn't even a woman. Yet with a heavy heart I knew there was no mistake, for if the aunt I remembered was no more, it was only because she had become what my mother and father had become in the end — broken on the earth like pieces of rotten wood by the cowardly greed of these hungry hills.

"This here paper, boy," she began, "was the will your mother made out before she passed on. I ain't got no quarrel with anyone, but she didn't know what become of you, or if you were ever coming back. So when we got her into town with the last attack, she called for the preacher Crowe and for a policeman to be her witnesses. The preacher didn't come, but the policeman made out this paper which she signed."

My aunt stuck the paper at me, and it trembled in her weak hand.

"Read it!"

I didn't want to read it. I knew what it said, so I pushed her hand away from me.

"With her own hand your mother signed this paper, and it says that this land and everything on it belongs to me, her sister," Aunt Matilda now had the will close to her face. "So if you're thinking of making any claims or moving me out, you'd just better know where you stand, Snit Mandolin!"

She leaned toward me, staring hard into my face.

"You've changed, Snit. You don't even look much like us Mandolins, and I don't like it. I don't know you no more."

The cold hostility and fear were fading from her eyes. But just as quickly, they became fired and intense with a hidden fever.

"Listen to me, Snit!" she said in a hoarse whisper. "If you

wanna work the place and help me out, I won't be saying anything to you, or asking you to go! Just so long as you don't intend making trouble. I don't want no trouble. But if you try starting anything first or behind my back, I'll grind you into dust! D'you understand?" She slammed her dry, small fist hard on the table. I looked at her, and saw that she was scared — real scared. I rose from my bench and walked to the door.

"Where you goin' now?" Aunt Matilda demanded in a shrill voice.

"I don't know," I replied, and stepped out into the sun-baked yard.

I wanted to have a smoke. Pete had given me cigarettes from the coffee-shop for nothing. I smoked very little, but now I felt I needed something to cheer me and take my mind off this desolation and suspicion. I crossed the yard to the road, and turned in the direction of the store.

The road felt quite warm under my feet even though it was still morning. My shoes sank into the loose dust, and became ashen-grey after a few steps. The sky was a roof of hot lead. There would be no rain this day — if anyone had asked me for an opinion, I would have said there would be no rain the rest of this summer. Yet the fields had some greenery to them — and the barley, though short in height, was turning a pale golden colour. But the pastures were dry and wilted.

I saw cows wandering over the parched earth in search of grazing grass, swishing the sandflies off their backs with their tails, and mooing sadly. I had never seen cattle so bony and hungry-looking before.

Short of Whittles' store, the road dipped and rose through a slight hollow. The air was cooler here, and I began to walk faster. A red-faced farmer, with a high thatch of grey hair on his head, was walking toward me with a shovel over his shoulder. He was grinning as he approached, but when he came near enough to see me, the smile faded from his face and he turned away from me. After I passed him, I turned quickly, and saw him hurrying away without a backward glance. I knew him — George Webster. "The Law of the Land," folks called him. That's because he always used this expression in an argument. Like the time Shnitka's Jersey cow broke pasture and wandered into Webster's yard. Webster tied a rope around its neck and led the cow back to Shnitka.

"The law of the land sez ya gotta keep your stock fenced in proper, Shnitka," Webster warned. "Don't let it happen again!"

George Webster had spent all his spare time wandering up and down the road to our community. He was a sort of one-man maintenance outfit, filling in deep ruts in the road and covering culverts with ditch clay so's the rain wouldn't get at them to rot them. In the spring he was busiest, for then he used to open up ditches to drain the run-off water.

"Ya must be a rich bugger, all the money ya make from the gov'ment on road work," someone would say.

Webster would look hard not only at the person who said that, but at the neighbours who stood around listening with grins on their faces.

"There are those who do their best to make life better, and there are others," he would say in a big voice. "I do what I can, and I do it for nothing. But the law of the land says all men are rewarded for their labours, and one day I will get paid."

"Maybe they'll give you a pension when you get old and shaky, and you'll end up being a somebody after all!" they would laugh, and Webster would walk away. Not because they made jokes at him, but because they spoke of old age, and George Webster was afraid of growing old. It bothered him. When Reverend Crowe gave a sorrowful sermon on the waste of passing life, folks listened thoughtfully, with their heads bent low. Except George Webster, who scratched at his heavy red neck, and ran his fingers through his white hair in fear.

He used to play catch-ball around the store on Sunday afternoons, and some mornings he could be seen running fast down the road, trying to keep the juices of youth high in his body.

He didn't marry. although folks had a story about how he tried. The story went that he used to buy magazines and answer the ads from lonely women that they contained. He was supposed to have received a letter of reply from some woman in Three Rivers, Quebec, in which she enclosed a picture of herself riding an elephant during her missionary days in India. My mother had seen the picture.

"She looks nice and young, but the picture itself is very old," mother said. "Besides, what's Webster want with a woman who rides elephants?"

Whether Webster had these same thoughts, or whether he had other thoughts of his own, he did not mail-order himself a wife, but remained single.

In my own way, I had felt pleased to see him. He was one of the many objects, dead and living, of home — like stones by the roadside, broken fences, cattle losing tufts of winter fur, a man limping with weariness, or a bunch of weed blown in a ball across a field. Yet he had not been pleased to see me, and this both amused and bothered me as I approached the general store.

A kid who grows up without a proper home or family grows up quickly. Early in life I had learned that a loud noise attracted attention from folks around me, those who liked me as well as those who didn't. So I pounded my heels hard on the short board walk that stuck out like a dry tongue from the doorway of Whittles' store in the direction of the road. The building was old and warped, with clapboard siding which had never been painted and was now the colour of the surrounding fields. I pushed the door open with difficulty, for it dragged on the floor.

I saw Whittles at the far end of the counter which stretched the length of the store. He was placing bars of laundry soap on a shelf. Even turned away from me as he was, I noticed he had become heavier since I last saw him.

I slammed the door shut with a bang, and Tom Whittles turned with a frown on his round face.

"Where in goddam hell do you think —" he began to say, then he saw me and the colour left his face. His lips were still open, but instead of speaking, he lifted his arm and pointed a pudgy finger in my direction, as if accusing me of something, or trying to order me out of the building.

"I wanna package of Exports," I said quietly.

For a long while he didn't move. Then the colour began creeping back into his cheeks and temples, and he took a step towards me, his finger still pointing in my direction.

"Gimme some cigarettes." I started to get sore. "Come on, I haven't got all day."

He reached the part of the counter directly in front of me now, and with a crooked smile twisting his face, he reached out to shake my hand.

"Snit! How are ya, boy? Sure glad to see ya back — so big and strong-looking! Boy! Ya've sure grown some!" His words tripped over one another like a bunch of clumsy pups learning to walk.

"Boy — will folks hereabouts be surprised and pleased when I tell them you're back, Snit! And wait 'til Reverend Crowe hears the news. Ya'll be a great help to us now, coming back from where it was ya were! Folks hereabouts, or what's left of them, have sorta drifted away from parish life!"

He turned to get my cigarettes. He was so rattled, the veins on the back of his neck twitched. To rattle him double, I paid him for the cigarettes by giving him the cheque which Pete had paid me with, and which I still had not cashed.

Tom Whittles picked it up and examined it closely, shaking his head with disbelief.

"I can't handle that, Snit — I haven't got stock in the store worth that much. Pay me some other time when ya've got smaller money," he said, handing the cheque back to me. I dug around in my pockets and found the right change for the cigarettes.

Whittles came from behind the counter to see me to the

door. I was about to leave when a thought came to mind.

"Say," I said, turning around, "I just remembered something! Reverend Crowe — that's the guy! He was the preacher who looked like you, and who busted his ass to get me sent away — also drove my Aunt Matilda nutty with his holy baloney."

The grin Whittles had managed to work up blew off as if I'd slapped him in the face. For a moment I thought he was going to burst into tears. He looked just like a big, fat kid who'd taken one helluva beating, and had nobody to tattle to.

"If ya'll be seeing Reverend Crowe soon, then tell him I said he can go fuck himself! And you, Whittles, go fuck yoreself too — twice!" I yanked the door out of his hand and slammed it as hard as I could.

Out on the road I felt good, like I could take on anything and come out a winner. Everything was sawdust and fear here in the hills. With three hundred bucks in my pocket I was accomplished, grown up and rich — and nobody was ever going to spit in my eye again.

The sun was rising fast now, and the morning had become hot and dusty. I walked off the powdery road, and found the tufts of grass growing near the ditch much cooler and more comfortable to the feet. When I reached the boundary of my aunt's farm, I did not go towards the house, but cut off to approach the buildings from behind, and so have a look at the fields.

These no longer reflected Aunt Matilda's industry. The land was badly plowed, and the barley she had sown was late and parched with improper cultivation. Weeds grew everywhere, and what harvest she would get this year wouldn't even pay for the binder twine she would have to purchase. I skirted the first hill and made my way to the pasture. There were only two cows, skinny and unfreshened. She had fenced off one corner of the pasture for the two horses she must have bought since I was away. They were in very bad condition, and were just now losing their winter shag. Worst of all, the four animals appeared to have had no water for a few days.

I opened the pasture gates, and they trotted towards the house and the watering-trough.

Walking after them in the direction of the farmstead, I tried to reckon on how much money would be required to get the farm functioning again, but all my planning only depressed me. I could easily see the three hundred dollars I carried being swallowed up with hardly a thing to show for the bother.

If only it would rain, then any gamble might pay off. I would get nowhere discussing my plans with Aunt Matilda, for her mind was dimmed now. There was no telling how she would react or how the best plans would be shadowed by the private terrors with which she lived.

The sky was milky, with a sun so hot it burned my naked arms and face as if a hot iron was held near the skin.

If only it would rain. . . .

five

I was tired, but I couldn't sleep. So I found a very old copy of the *Family Herald and Weekly Star* in the rubbish under my bed and brought it to the kitchen to read. Aunt Matilda was sitting in front of the kitchen stove, peering at the flames which showed through a crack in the burning chamber. She was rocking back and forth in her chair, nodding her head to a maddening, constant rhythm. The heat of the stove combined with the warmth of the sunscorched walls to make the room almost unbearable.

I opened the buttons of my soggy shirt, and putting my feet on the kitchen table, settled down to read. My aunt turned her face from the stove and studied my feet for a while, then her gaze moved to my face. I could feel her looking at me — her stare seemed to give off a peculiar heat of its own, which made the moisture run from my hair down the back of my neck.

"Whatcha staring at me for?" I muttered, but got no reply. I looked up at her, and noticed with shock that her eyes were blank and mirror-like, almost like the eyes of a cat peering into light. She hadn't heard me — I don't think she was even aware I was in the room. All the same, I felt uneasy and brought my feet off the table.

There was a knock on the door, and I almost jumped out of my chair. Aunt Matilda also came out of her reverie, and a scowl darkened her thin face.

"You expecting someone?" she asked me suspiciously, but made no move to open the door.

"Yeh, yeh — I'm expecting the Prime Minister to drop in for a cup of coffee!" I said testily, for I was finding her moods and suspicions just a bit wearing. She was queer, in a way which scared me and made me mad all at the same time. The knock came again, stronger now, and Aunt Matilda rose to her feet. Wrapping her head scarf about her shoulders, even though the night was a living heat, she left for her bedroom, closing the door after her. I felt bad for having spoken mean to her, and got up to go after her and apologize. But the knock came again.

"Hi, Snit — ya sleepin?" Johnny Swift stepped through the door I had opened, and blinked his eyes at the kitchen lamp.

"Sit down." I waved my hand to the chair Aunt Matilda had sat in. He was sweating in great beads which rolled down the sides of his face and gathered in the pink folds of his throat.

"How ya doin', kid?" He grinned up at me as I found two cups and poured tea for both of us. He drank his cupful with one gulp and pushed it out for a refill.

"You gonna bugger up your liver drinkin' that fast," I said.

He looked at me with surprise. "I didn't know that. Where's a guy's liver anyhow?" I didn't know. He drank his second cupful with less haste and sat back in his chair and rolled himself a cigarette. "Anyone else in?" — he motioned towards my aunt's bedroom. I nodded and he scraped his chair nearer the table.

"Snit, whatcher plannin' to do here?" he asked almost casually as if it didn't concern him, but his voice was low and secretive now and his eyes were excited. "This backwoods farm don't even buy ya clothes for yore ass."

"I reckon it don't at that. I just haven't made up my mind about anything, Johnny." He took a long puff on a cigarette, watching me, then he leaned forward in his chair, his eyes narrow.

"I wanna talk to ya, Snit — but ya gotta promise nobody don't hear what I say. I got a few things goin' for hard cash, but ya gotta keep as tight as a nail in a board about it — like my old man. He has a good idea what's goin' on, but I told him I'd snap his head off his neck if he squealed, and he don't tell anyone the time of day since. So ya gotta promise to keep it under yore hat!"

The lamplight flared between us for a moment and then fell to its faint yellow glow. In that light, I got a very good look at Johnny Swift. When I rode in from town with him a few days ago, I had somehow thought his face still had the softness of childhood about it. But I was wrong, very wrong. The soft babyish fat I thought I had seen about his cheekbones was gone. In its place he had the loose flesh which comes of not sleeping properly.

He seemed round and deceptively gentle, but his deeply imbedded eyes were sharp and hard. Yet this was a contradiction of his manner, which was boyish and awkward. His easy, mischievous smile — the fine fuzz on his cheeks and all the dirt — suggested a good-natured boy. But sitting across the kitchen table from me now was another Johnny Swift — a darker man who was growing up below the surface of skin and cloth.

I had seen his face before, on a spark-plug salesman who came to the garage one day and sold Pete three cartons of defective plugs, which we had to spill into a garbage bucket when car owners we sold the first sets to returned with complaints. This same salesman was arrested ten months later attempting to hold up a supermarket in Calgary. I saw his pciture in the paper — a nice, round-faced, jolly sort of fellow you can grow up with and never know a thought going through his head.

"You know me, Johnny. Whatcha got in mind?" I asked.

"It's this way, Snit," Johnny looked sideways at Aunt Matilda's door. "Ya can't make any pocket dough growin' barley, milkin' cows or raisin' stupid hogs. An' if ya don't have hard cash in yore pocket, ya don't have a goddamn thing! Now you've been around. Them places ya been to ain't no church picnics — although it's in jail a guy really gets to know which end is up. That damned Tom Whittles is blowin' his wind about how he seen a three-hundred-buck-cheque on ya. When I heard that, I thought to myself, 'Old Snit's been around — he knows the ropes!' So I come down to talk to ya, and see what I could do to help ya."

His cigarette had gone out. As he relit with another match, which he struck against the leg of his pants, I noticed his face sweating until his cheeks seemed to crawl with moisture. His jaw was closed tight, and little muscles in the upper parts of his throat twitched with nervousness.

"I got some cash, Snit. I ain't got no three hundred bucks like you got. But I got some stashed away that my old man nor nobody else in these parts knows about — because I'm smart, and I ain't gonna show my hand and have questions asked about me. Ya understand, don't ya, Snit?"

I didn't know what the hell he was talking about, and told him so. He cleared his throat and leaned forward until I could feel his hot breath on my face.

"I'm in moonshine, boy — right up to here!" he said in a voice hardly more than a whisper, and indicating his neck with a dirty finger.

"What are ya saying? Ya making and peddling the stuff?"

He nodded with a sly smile.

"How in hell — don't the mounties get on to ya?"

Johnny wiped his brow with his arm.

"Ya're damned right they know it's being made and sold in a pretty big way. But how they gonna nail me? I got a good head on me — they don't know who makes the stuff. So they're sittin', waitin' for me to make a wrong move. They can't get me movin' the stuff out, 'cause they'd have to go through every wagon of cream cans and potatoes the local yokels haul into town. If they missed on the first wagon they searched, they'd miss on all the others — you know how word travels when somethin' happens! An' the day they start searchin' wagons, Johnny Swift's wagon is gonna turn around and go home. Oh no, Corporal Kane has more upstairs than to go searchin' folks. Ya know what's he waitin' for?"

I admitted I didn't.

"They're waitin' for me to flash the cash. Ya know — like goin' into town and buyin' a pair of expensive horses at my age — or a better piece of farm machinery instead of the second-hand junk everyone here deals in. The cops know how much a man can buy farmin' gumbo in the hills, so if someone one day shows up with a couple hundred in pocket, they got him marked just like that! Then all Corporal Kane and his clucks gotta do is wait a coupla days — then take an easy drive to yore place one night and nip ya distillin' the stuff by the creek. Then bingo — three hundred bucks in fines, or ya go to jail, and some punk cop gets a pat on the head!"

"I still don't see what yore driving at." I was getting sore, because I didn't see what he was leading up to.

"I could use ya, Snit." Johnny's face was white now and strained with worry. "Folks know ya came with cash on ya — Whittles seen to that already. So why don't ya give me a hand in turnin' out and hawkin' the damned stuff? All ya gotta do is carry the cash on ya, and do any buyin' we make. Cops get nosy, and folks say, 'Oh yeh, the kid's been away three years and come back with a wad — lucky bugger!' So the cops get their noses off ya. Meanwhile, we save up and work as anybody else does durin' the day. When we got enough saved up, we light out and start some business of our own — and ta hell with the hills and all the ass-holes in 'em! Nobody can touch us then! Whatcha say, Snit?"

Everything he said came so hot and fast I had to think about it for a while, trying to foresee difficulties for us in a partnership of this kind. His ideas made sense all right. The land wouldn't grow wild grass in a dry year, least of all proper grain. As far as my future here with my Aunt Matilda went, I had about as much chance as a hog in a stonepile. Even trying to fatten the cattle for milk or meat was pretty hopeless and would chew up all the money I carried in no time flat.

"I'd like to think it over, Johnny," I said. "How do you think we gonna get on with one another — like, who's to see we don't try to do one another for the money we make?"

Johnny seemed disappointed.

"I dunno, Snit — whatever ya think is best by us is okay with me. I ain't aimin' to cheat ya. Ya wanna go fifty-fifty, we can split anythin' we get. I got some supplies but that don't matter — I ain't gonna charge ya for comin' in."

I could see Johnny was being pressed for someone to cover up, and I could drive any sort of deal I wanted. But the fifty-fifty split seemed okay by me. Johnny was as sweaty as an old horse now, what with not being sure if I was going along or not. He got up from his chair and came toward me with an outstretched hand. I shook it, and found his palm dead and sticky.

"Snit — if ya back out, ya promise ya won't say to nobody I saw ya?" he asked.

"Naw — don't worry!"

"Ya don't think the old crow heard us, do ya?" He pointed with his head to my aunt's bedroom door.

"Naw — she's out of it, probably asleep."

"Okay, Snit. Think it over and keep yore lips shut. I'll be out on the road tomorrow at this time, and ya can come and tell me what ya aim to do."

He left in a hurry, forgetting to close the kitchen door behind him.

I blew out the light and went outside to have a piss. The night was warm, and frogs croaked from the pond like they croaked all through my childhood. Only now I could smell the pond for what it had become — a small puddle of rotten, heavy mud. A slight wind blew across the hills from the west, and it had the same dry odour of scorched vegetation I had first noticed when I came into town on my return.

Only now it seemed stronger.

Next morning I ate a bowl of coarse cereal, and rose from the table immediately after to go out into the fields.

"Whatcha doin' now?" Aunt Matilda looked up from the table. She hadn't touched her food. I felt raw and edgy, and in no mood for company over an after-breakfast coffee.

"Nothin' — just goin' out," I said over my shoulder.

"If you're over for anything with Johnny Swift, then mind your step. He's a bad little bugger," my aunt warned.

It was still an early hour, but a brisk wind had started up. The short grain stalks had the dew blown off them even though the sun was still low over the hills to the east and the fields were in shadow.

I hadn't been able to sleep much for thinking about how I would work the harvest this summer. As I walked through the field, I pinched the forming heads on the barley and oats, but discovered only bran. The odd time when my thumbnail cut into a forming kernel of grain, it was pasty and small, and would not pay for the cutting and binding of it, not to mention the cost of threshing. I could see no other way out but to cut all the grain for hay and save money and labour later. In this way, it would at least provide the cattle and horses with roughage for the winter ahead.

When I reached the pasture, I tried to catch the horses. But I was strange to them, and they gave me a strong chase around the field. Both of them had halters on their heads, but no sooner I got within reach of their heads, they would snort and run from me. I finally cornered the older of the two — a large-hooved and lame Percheron. As I led him out of the pasture and towards the farm buildings, the other one followed. Quickly I got them into the barn and harnessed. On the way out, I took them to the well and gave them water. The well was in the yard in front of the house, and Aunt Matilda saw me. She came out and approached me, a puzzled expression on her face.

"What are you doing, Snit?" she asked sharply, her hands clutching at her coat.

"Hitching the team up to the mower and cutting down the grain for hay. It won't pay to keep it out there growin'," I replied.

"Snit Mandolin!" she exclaimed. "You get them harnesses off and stop your mucking about!"

"Listen, Aunt Matilda — I wanna tell ya —"

"Don't you go tellin' me nothing I don't know! There'll be rain in a few days, and the crop will come out strong and good as ever — so don't go ruining things! There'll be rain — you know there'll be rain! An' what right you got to go cutting *my* grain down without my say-so? I didn't ask you to come around with your high-flown ideas. I'm born to the land and worked to put that grain down while you were city-slickin' about! Now just take them harnesses off the horses and clear off — you hear me?"

She was shaking all over with anger, her eyes burning like she had a powerful fever, and her yellow-white hair hanging in loose strands about her bony shoulders. Her withered little hands were clenched into tight fists, which she raised toward me. She was of the land, all right — she proved it to me, for I could never feel this strongly about the goddamned dust and everything that grew out of it. But I also knew she was wrong; she was like a blind dog walking into a building which is burning up, not realizing every step in the direction he chooses brings him one step nearer to death and destruction. I thought of the bony, hunger-mooing cattle in the pasture.

"Shut up, Aunt Matilda! Get back into the house and stay there!" I didn't raise my voice, for I wasn't angry with her. I just had to get past her.

She stared at me in an odd sort of way, with her mouth open as if she were planning to say something, but didn't know where to begin. Then a cloud came over her sparkling eyes, and she turned quickly and went back into the house.

I led the horses back of the field shed, where the old mower had been left in a jungle of pig-weed and thistle. I examined the blades and found them rusted from exposure to the weather, but as I didn't have a file or sandpaper to clean them with, I proceeded to hitch the horses to the machine and try working it in the condition it was. When I pushed the clutch in, the mower did work, but it was hard pulling for the horses.

The farm had little sown to grain — only about forty acres in all, and half of the fields were hills, where the soil was sandy and hot and nothing except the hardiest weeds grew. So I cut the lower patches where there was some ground moisture and the grain grew as tall as a foot in some places. But it was slow work, for I had to stop often to rest the badly fed, lathery horses. When the sun rose high the sand-flies blackened the air, giving the horses as much bother as pulling the sluggish mower did.

I scraped some grease off the mower axles and dabbed the mess around the noses of the animals, to keep the flies out. But it didn't do much good, and the horses suffered, with me not able to help them.

It took the best part of the day to get the cutting done. By now the lame Percheron was limping badly, and his smaller companion was dropping behind. But with the falling of the sun low over the hills to the west, the air cooled, for which I was grateful, because my neck and head ached with heat exposure. Then I cut through the last swath, and disengaging the mower, turned the stumbling, snorting horses toward the shed where the machine had been stored. Unhitching them, I led them back to the barn to remove their harnesses and brush them down. I found a bucket and went to the grain bin to get some oats for them.

The bin was empty, and the floor was littered with mouse droppings. So I took the horses back to pasture, and watching them walk away to graze, low-headed and weary, I cursed the futility of life.

"Goddamit!" I thought aloud. "If Johnny Swift got an easier way for a man to live in these parts, then I go the way of Johnny Swift. A man's gotta eat to live, and there won't be much eating from the work I do on this farm!"

The house was in darkness when I approached. Inside, the kitchen stove was cold and still held the pans and dishes of the morning meal. I lit the lamp and kindled the stove, then washed my face and head in cold water. Then I set about making a supper of fried eggs and tea.

The door to Aunt Matilda's bedroom was closed, and when I opened it, I saw her lying face downward on her bed.

"I got supper done," I told her. "Come on and eat with me."

She began sobbing into her pillow, and I approached her.

"Don't you hear me, Aunt Matilda — supper's ready."

I shook her by the shoulder, and she turned, fixing her red-rimmed eyes on my face. Then she rose quickly on an elbow and spat at me, after which she dropped her head back into the pillow and continued sobbing. I jumped back, feeling a disgust and a pity for her.

"I done what I thought was right — there's no other way," I stammered, but she lifted her hands to cover her ears.

I lost my stomach for food, and hurried outside and up the road to meet Johnny Swift.

The road was dark and silent. I stood listening, but all I could hear was the chirping of crickets on the hillsides.

"Johnny! Where ya hiding?" I called, but got no reply. I couldn't wait any longer — I had to find Johnny, so I ran north towards the Swift farm.

Johnny's place was two farms down from us, next to the Rogers', whose land bordered on Aunt Matilda's. Rogers and my aunt did not share a common boundary fence, however, for the road allowance ran between these two farms. The road itself had never been cut through, for the land on the far side away from the highway on which I hurried was wild, and nobody ever had reason to explore on the west side of all the farms which hung on the market road.

I was aiming to run all the way to the Swift farm, but I only got as far as the road allowance, for Johnny was waiting for me there. He was riding a horse, and holding another by the lead.

"Johnny!"

"Where in hell ya been this long? Thought ya'd never come," he said peevishly. The horses were restless, and turned circles on the dark, dusty road.

"I come as fast as I could."

"What's yore answer, Snit — ya comin' with me, or aintcha?" Johnny leaned towards me, but I could not see his face.

"Sure, I'm with ya, Johnny! All the way!"

"Get on!"

I mounted the spare horse. Before I could ask him where we were going, Johnny turned off the road into the overgrown road allowance, and rode west at a fast trot.

Johnny's still was set up in back of his father's farm, in a heavy clump of alder which grew where a bog had been in wetter years. It was impossible to walk through this jungle from the field side of the Swift farm, so we had to ride a detour some two miles long over the road allowance and then back to the bog through an abandoned farm which was now overgrown with bush.

"Why in hell didn't we walk through Roger's farm?" I asked Johnny as I pulled my horse alongside his.

"Too risky," he said, glancing back over his shoulder. "Never know when Rogers might be creepin' around his farm — lookin' for mushrooms, maybe!"

Johnny laughed at his joke, but I didn't see anything funny. As soon as we left the road allowance and began back-tracking over the deserted farm, the horses seemed to follow instinctively a faint path through the waste and shrub. Reaching thicker bushes, Johnny stopped and dismounted.

"Okay, Snit — we tie the nags here and go the rest of the way on foot. Gets pretty soft ahead." And he led the way for the remaining distance.

Then we reached the place — a scooped-out hollow, completely overhung by alder branches. It was pitch dark here, musty and heavy with the smell of yeast and fermentation, Johnny lit a storm lantern and quickly draped a sack over it, so that only a thin panel of light shone on his equipment.

"Cripes! What a set-up!" I exclaimed, seeing the still and the fermentation cans.

"Yeh — nothin' can go wrong! Even if somebody was stupid enough to come here, he'd have to walk right in on my factory to find it. An' look at them branches, Snit — ya see any stars through them?"

I looked up, but could see nothing through the heavy alder branches and leaves.

"Even if the cops was birds they'd never spot me!" Johnny said with pride. Then he set about lighting a fire under the nearest fermenting-drum. As the flames caught, I saw his face in the flickering light. It was soaking with sweat, which gathered in little pools at the edges of his tightly closed lips.

He stood up and handed a bucket to me. "Here. About ten steps back through there ya'll find a water-hole. It smells like shit, but it's cold, and we gotta have cold water for the cooler. Fill up the bucket, and I'll set up the gear."

I found the pool all right, and Johnny hadn't exaggerated about how stagnant it was. When I returned, he had set up everything and was working a low, well-controlled fire under the distilling drum. I emptied the water I had brought into the cooling trough, and stood by watching him.

"Ya gotta have the fire just so. Make it too low, and ya steam all the booze off. Too high, and it pukes the yeast all through the fuckin' lines. Get the empties under the line."

I placed one empty gallon jug under the end of the long copper pipe which stuck out of the far side of the cooler. I then set a couple of other jugs beside the first one. After this I waited, while Johnny fanned the fire and used the same leafy branch to break up the smoke.

It took over an hour for the mash to come to a boil, and for the first trace of liquid to show at the end of the copper tube. When the first drops of alcohol formed, Johnny threw down the branch he was waving and feverishly crouched down to watch the whiskey drain.

"Come on, baby!" he whispered. "Ataboy! Faster, and pure as tears! Come on, baby!"

I too was burning with excitement now — the hot feeling that something was happening to turn my life into a new and happier time.

It was still dark when we finished distilling, but a lot of

work remained to be done. Even though the drum was boiling hot, Johnny worked at disconnecting the tubing, cursing softly as he burned his hands. Finally he got the nut undone, and we rolled the hot drum to one side off the stand. Johnny crouched down and disappeared into the underbrush, returning a moment later with a shovel.

"Hurry up — dig a hole!" He handed the shovel to me. As I dug into the soft earth, he unscrewed the top off the drum. The smell of the boiled mash was sickening. I turned my face away and choked for breath.

"C'mon — what's the holdup? This ain't no fancy party, Snit — we got to git outa here before it lights up!" Johnny's voice was threatening.

When I opened a hole about a foot deep and two feet wide, Johnny said that would do, and he worked the drum toward me. When he had it over the edge of the hole, he turned it over and drained the mash out of it.

"Cover it, quick!" he whispered thickly. "I'll wash up and reload."

I was fascinated by his organization and timing. Slow and clumsy as he seemed, he was a transformed person here in his moonshine den. Very quickly he had the drum scraped and sponged, and was refilling it with ground grain which he had hidden previously in a sack under some moss. He rolled the drum back on its stand, and then dumped a bag of sugar and some dry yeast over the crushed grain. He disappeared in the underbrush again, this time returning dragging a cream can full of fresh water. He emptied this water into the drum, and then stirred the mixture with a stick.

"If ya wanna drink, then wait until ya get home. I had to bring this water in my arms, ridin' a horse. If ya think that's fun — ya'll get a chance to do it next time," he said grimly.

A few more shovelsful of dirt, and I finished covering the refuse. Johnny was already winding up operations by reconnecting the distilling pipe to the drum. But instead of replacing the steel screw-on cap on the drum itself, he merely tied a piece of cheesecloth over the top.

"The stuff's gotta breathe while it ferments," he said,

looking up to see me watching him.

While I drained the water from the cooling trough, he cleaned up the area around the drum by replacing the shovel and cream can into the underbrush. We capped the two jugs of moonshine and put them in the empty grain sack. Johnny stamped out the last traces of hot embers under the stand; then he hoisted the sack over his shoulder and, motioning to me to follow him, led the way back to where he had left the horses.

"Goddammit, Snit, it's later than I thought it was!" he swore as we came out on the road allowance. "Let's git out on the double before some early shepherd finds us here!"

Despite the brush and treacherous ground of the abandoned farm, we galloped back towards the settlement. Dawn was coming fast now, and even before we reached the first bend in the trail and were heading directly east to where our ways would part, the sky was turning grey. I could faintly pick out the outlines of the hills around us, with their narrow fields and clusters of brush and wood.

At the main road I dismounted and gave the bridle leads to Johnny. I was startled to see how pale and moist he looked in the ghostly grey light of early morning. He was also irritable and in no mood to hang about.

"Go home, Snit — hurry up! An' hang yore shirt on the fence to air, or the smell of it is a giveaway. I'll call fer ya later today on the way to town. Got to get some groceries. Git the hell indoors! I'll see ya later."

I stood for a moment watching his departure, and taking a deep breath of the dust his horses had thrown up as he wheeled them sharply and trotted away in the direction of his farm.

Walking the remaining distance home, I felt very tired. I didn't want to undress, so instead of going into the house, I walked into the barn. It was still dark in the building. I fumbled trying to locate the ladder leading into the hayloft. When I did find it, I pulled myself up.

There was still a layer of old timothy hay in the loft. Finding the first convenient spot, I lay down and fell asleep almost immediately.

On the way into town, Johnny brought me up to date on the history of the countryside. He told me of those who died, and he told me of those who had found a new foothold on life, and of the others who failed in spirit and health. He also told of those who had married, colouring his observations with his own cynical attitude towards life and love. There were some girls who had become unwed mothers, and these gave him great amusement.

"Lots of hot potatoes here, Snit boy!" He roared, and slapped his knee so hard the horses jumped forward and almost toppled me off my seat. "They'd give it to a trapper, and they'd give it to a cowboy!"

He laughed again, nudging me in the side with his elbow.

"Y'ever had anything to do with a girl?" I asked.

"Naw — that stuff's not fer me. A woman only ruins a man. If she don't give him a pile of kids, she gives him other troubles," he said darkly.

"What kind of troubles?"

He looked down and dragged his feet back and forth across the floor of the wagon before answering.

"Hell, I coulda got married if I wanted to, Snit — any time I wanted to, I coulda married. But what's it get ya? Ya get married to one of 'em, and they start to bugger around with some other guy. Jesus, I get mad when I think of it. I could kill the whole goddamned bunch of 'em for it!"

"Ya sound like that preacher Crowe," I growled.

"Don't mix me up with no preacher, if ya know what's good for ya!" He was getting sore. "I don't believe in no God!"

"What makes you sound like you know what's right and wrong about everything?"

"All right! So I don't know nothin'. But I got my eyes open — I see what I see. If ya want to go around thinkin' folks is all made of holy shit, that's yore tough luck! Me,

I look out fer myself — and don't ya forget it!"

He got pretty gloomy after that, and we didn't speak for the longest time.

The two whiskey jugs were wrapped in a horse blanket in the back of the wagon. I turned to look at them often, worrying if they should overturn and smash. Johnny seemed to have forgotten about them altogether.

We were passing a farm which was distinctive in that it had a fence around the front yard. A man was at the well, drawing up water for a flock of noisy geese. Johnny saw him, and grinned.

"Hello, Joe — waddaya know?" he called.

The farmer took one hand off the bucket rope he was pulling and waved to us.

"Who's he?" I asked.

"Joe Skrypka — ya must've known him. He married a French girl from the other side of town — hell, I guess that was after you were gone," Johnny said cheerfully, as if our argument had never taken place. "Yeh, she had quite a time of it — I figured it would drive Joe to the bug-house."

"Was there something wrong with her?"

"Yeh — she had cancer, and never told Joe about it. It was only after she had a kid Joe found out. Too late to do anythin' by that time."

"Is she still around?" I asked.

"Naw — she died over a year ago. Joe's old lady is takin' care of the kid. Sure changed Joe."

"What ya mean?"

"Well, he went sorta crazy after that. Figures his old lady is his wife — even calls her Jeanette, which was what his wife was called. Some of the neighbours told the old woman she should get him packed off to a nuthouse. But she figures he can't do no harm bein' around, and if he was taken off, the farm would go to pot — so ya got yer choice!"

"Cripes!"

As we passed the next farm, a dog bounded out after us. He ran alongside of our wagon and set up one helluva racket barking. Johnny had been driving this far, but now he passed the leads to me. Then quickly leaning over the edge of the wagon, he caught hold of the dog's tail.

The dog yelped with fear and pain, and Johnny lifted him clear off his feet and began swinging him in a circle round and round over his head. The horses got jumpy at the noise over their backs, and I had to hold tight to keep them from breaking into a frightened trot. When Johnny got the howling dog into a fast spin, he let go of the tail and the poor devil went sailing over the edge of the road, across a barbed-wire fence, and head-on into a thicket of scrub willows on the other side.

"That's one sonofabitch won't bother me no more. Been waitin' to do that fer a long time, but never had anyone around to hold the horses from boltin'," Johnny said with satisfaction as he took the leads from me.

The hot air seemed to rise from the pores of the earth, to meet the burning sun overhead. Holding on to my seat with both hands, I tried to keep my head from nodding, for the low rumble and the jogging of the wagon were putting me to sleep. Johnny must have been bothered in the same way, for he stopped talking until we got into town.

"Hey, Snit!" He stabbed at me with his elbow as we lumbered down the main street. "I'm gonna have ya hang onto our money. But don't go showin' it to anyone. Ya just hold onto it, and keep count on how we spend it, but don't go flashin' no bills, Y'understand?"

I nodded, and Johnny steered the team towards the Grain Growers elevator.

He drove right on the scales in the building and let out a shout. In a moment the fat, stubble-bearded elevator agent came out of his office. scowling with heat and sleepiness. When he saw Johnny he smiled a dirty, rotten-tooth smile.

Johnny just sat, as if he didn't see the man. The agent first walked to the door of the elevator, and took a long look up and down the street. Then he walked to the back of our wagon, dug under the blanket, and took out the two moonshine jugs. He again looked out into the street, then furtively carried the jugs into his office. When he returned, he carried two identical but empty jugs under his arm. He placed them in the back of the wagon where the other two had been. Then coming over to Johnny, he dug into his pocket and gave him a handful of money.

"Get going, ya little bastard!" he said by way of parting, and hurried back into his office. We drove out of the building. As we reached the sunlit street, Johnny passed the money to me. I counted thirty dollars and pocketed them.

"Is that all there's to it?" I asked with wonder.

"We're homefree again, boy," Johnny said with satisfaction, although I could tell he was nervous as hell, the way he kept looking up and down the street. There were a few people about, but nobody paid us any interest.

"What's the score with prettyboy — he a bootlegger?" I asked, thumbing back at the elevator.

"Look, Snit — he don't ask me no questions, and I don't ask him none. It's best that way," Johnny said philosophically.

We pulled up at the hardware store and the horses snorted to clear their noses of dust.

"I want ya to do somethin', Snit," Johnny was staring past me, but talking fast and clear. "We only got a few months left for brewin' the poison. I got lots of copper pipe stashed away, but I can't go buyin' too many cream cans without someone gettin' suspicious. Especially since folks know I don't keep no milk cows. But it's different with you. Go and get two or three big cans, the eight-gallon kind, and we can expand our business. They won't make as good brewin' drums as the screw-top I have, but I got that one at an auction, and luck don't shit twice in the same place. Okay?"

I understood, and went into the store while Johnny waited for me. I got the two cream cans all right.

"How often you going to need these?" the hardware man asked as he reached up to pull them off a display shelf.

I almost got panicky, but his back was turned, and he didn't see me.

"Uh — once a week." I tried to sound as cheerful as possible.

"You got better luck than most other farmers in these parts, son — hardly any of 'em selling milk or cream this summer."

"I got some alfalfa hay from last year. They sure milk good on alfalfa!"

He wrote up a sales bill and I paid him. Then I picked up the two cans and made my way out. I glanced up and saw the bank sign next door, and a thought came to me.

"You wait here," I said to Johnny as I loaded the cream cans on the wagon. Then I went into the bank. Even here there was a delay I hadn't expected.

The girl at the wicket took Pete's cheque and went to the manager's office at the back. A moment later she returned.

"Mr. Mandolin, would you be able to call back in about a a half hour? We'll have to telephone Edmonton about your cheque."

"But why? What's wrong?"

"Oh, there's nothing wrong. Only, it's a personal cheque and we must find out if the account it is written on is still in existence. Perhaps twenty minutes . . .".

We left the horses in the shade of the hardware store and walked around town for a while. Pretty soon we got thirsty, and stopped outside Elsie's place. She was asleep as always, standing with her back to the mirror. The sun burned through the unshaded windows, and Johnny cursed.

"Damned if I go in there and roast for a cup of her slop!"

He rapped his knuckles sharply against the café window, which made Elsie jump and shake her fist at us. Johnny laughed, and we crossed over to the bank.

The cheque was good, and as I counted my money, the girl at the wicket watched me.

"If you'd like to deposit some money in an account . . ." she began to say, and I hesitated. But Johnny nudged me from behind.

"Don't leave no money in a bank, Snit! Don't ever do it!" he said grimly.

"Why, Johnny? No sense carting all this cash around."

"Yore crazy if ya leave it here. Everybody knows yore business then. And look at this damned place — could go up in smoke anytime, and all yore money with it! Banks are all right fer them as needs 'em — but I'd stay outa them if I was you!"

I didn't want to argue with the girl listening to us, so I thanked her and we went out.

The sun was a great red ball of dry heat when we started for home. Once we were out of town and no one to see, I took my shirt off. It didn't feel any cooler, but it amused Johnny.

"Jesus! — What'ya do — wash yerself all over every day? Ya look like ya was powdered all over, so white and clean! Betcha smell like a woman!"

And he nudged me in good fun, and laughed one of those laughs that bubbles out of a man's nose. I had a lot to say to him about this subject, but what was the use? So I endured, and kept silent.

six

August came, and still the weather continued dry and hot. The fields baked and cracked in many places, in long, snaking crevices many inches deep. The smell of dry leaves vanished from the wind, and a new, weaker scent, as of old leather, replaced it. Some forest fires had started far to the north, and we had a few cooler days when the smoke overcast the sky, screening out the sun.

I got the hay cured and stored in the hayloft. Also, I worked on some of the fences which needed new posts and wire-mending. I even persuaded Aunt Matilda to give up on the garden, for every plant had been scorched and dead since June, yet she had been persisting in hoeing and watering the wasted earth.

"Nothin' ever dies altogether — there's always a seed or root that lives, Snit. If you were a proper farmer, you'd know that yourself," she argued, before she finally gave up hope herself.

On one of my trips into town with Johnny, I purchased a load of feed oats from the elevator, much to the agent's surprise and Johnny's annoyance. Johnny was no farmer, and looked on my attempts to preserve and improve farm animals as a fool's dream.

"Whatcha wastin' money on a couple of bone dry cows fer? Cost ya more to fatten 'em than they're worth!" he chided.

He was right, but I felt sorry for the animals, but how could I explain this to Johnny Swift?

When we pulled into the yard and unloaded the oats into the feed shed, my aunt came out to see what we were up to.

"Why glory be!" she said. "How much is this costin', Snit? You didn't go borrowin' money from folks, didya?"

Johnny snickered, and began shovelling the grain into the shed.

"Here, now — let me give a hand!" My aunt climbed on the wagon, and turning up the frayed cuffs of her coat, took the shovel from Johnny. This was the first time I had seen her cheerful since my return.

Inside the barn, in one of the stalls at the very back, my father, or someone before him, had stored a small, single-cylinder John Deere stationary engine. When Johnny left, I pulled the motor out into the yard to dismantle and clean. When I got it together again, I filled the fuel tank with lamp kerosene. It took some time to start, but when I got it going I found it still worked reasonably well. Using it for a source of power, I was able to grind the grain I had bought.

That same evening, Aunt Matilda enthusiastically began feeding the two cows and caring for them properly again. She curried them, and they shied away at such unfamiliar attention.

She talked to me as I stood watching her. "You're a good lad, Snit. You've got a good heart and your head's set on right. I'd kinda given up hope when you took to chumming about with that good-for-nothing Swift boy — figured he'd take you for what money you had before the summer was over. Worse still, I figured he'd start movin' in on me. He's a bad one, Snit — I don't know how a soul deals with someone like him."

"Johnny's all right, Aunt Matilda. He ain't no better nor

worse than other folks in these parts. Everybody gets pushed into some kind of shape when times get tough — and ya know yourself times couldn't get no worse than they are."

"Bad times don't make people bad, Snit. People do queer things that maybe they'd rather forget later on. But it don't make them mean and bad. Somehow the bad ones start that way, and don't ever change."

"Then yo're saying everybody's good and kind as hell around here, and Johnny Swift is the one black bird in the country?"

My aunt didn't reply. She had stopped currying, and was watching me. Her little mouth was set angry, and her eyes were hard.

"Look," I continued, "I ain't got no quarrel with Johnny Swift. But I got a lot of quarrel with Tom Whittles, and the parson, and all them good folks that busted us up."

"Have you?" my aunt cut in sharply.

"What's the matter with ya?" I raised my voice at her. "Look at what they done to pa and ma! Look what they done to you! I was scared of ya, when I first saw ya! That's what all this nice, neighbourly treatment we been getting done to you."

"We done it ourselves, Snit — don't you see?" There were tears in Aunt Matilda's eyes now. "We done it long ago, and other folks had no part of it — it started long ago, when two sisters and a brother came on this farm. There was no proper life for anyone when the work was done. But instead of going out and doing what we shoulda done, saving ourselves for a good life, we turned ourselves inside out, killing everything we touched until we didn't know what was right or wrong any more. Your pa and ma paired off, and you were born. I was one of the outside folks then, and I hada start taking care of things. I coulda been like your ma — could've come and gone in the same way — just like your pa did. I was saved for a taste of life — but it come too late, Snit!"

I stood like a man that's been hit hard on the head but can't fall down. I thought of nothing — nothing at all. The only feeling I had was as if suddenly the soles of my feet had burst, draining all the blood and warmth out of me. When I became aware of my surroundings again, it was dark, and I heard Aunt Matilda weeping softly near the feeding cattle. I moved towards her, and lifted her to her feet.

"Has everybody known this — all these years?" I asked her as I held her close to myself.

"Yes, everybody has known."

"And nobody told — when the time come they sent out a petition."

Aunt Matilda nodded.

"We didn't do right by ourselves, and we didn't do right by you. Maybe it was best you got taken away. But you ruined it by comin' back. Why did you have to come back?"

I didn't know.

"I reckon we all have to go some place — and outside of Pete's garage, this is the only spot I've ever lived in," I said for want of something better to say.

"You're not sore about — everything?"

"No, Aunt Matilda; I'm not sore."

"You're not hurt too bad?"

I didn't say anything.

"All them things I said when I wasn't thinking, Snit — I take them back. If you're thinking of staying on with me, I'd like to talk to you —"

"It's late, Aunt Matilda — yo're tired. Let's go in."

There was nothing to discuss about my presence on the farm. I was going to pay my own way, but at the same time I didn't feel rooted here, and I would make no commitments,

Then there was Johnny. She must never learn of my association with him, for she was a good and honest woman — and for that very reason I could no longer trust her.

Our nights were busy. There was little to do on the farm, so Aunt Matilda did not miss me while I slept during the days. I had taken to sleeping in the barn hayloft, so that she would not become concerned or suspicious about my movements. The way I figured it, even if she caught me sleeping, she would think I was lazy or bothered by the heat.

Johnny was a terror for brewing. Each night he would haul in more containers of various sizes and shapes and fill them with mash for fermenting, until we had enough of the stuff going to produce about fifty gallons of moonshine. We had worked out a system for placing away so much fresh mash per night, and when the fermentation matured, distilling the containers in rotation. Because of this extra volume, we soon ran short of the finely ground barley and wheat which we used for raw mash.

"What we gonna do?" I asked, when we emptied the last bag of prepared grain.

"What we gonna do? I'll tell ya what we gonna do. I'm gonna see that punk elevator guy, and get him to grind and mix some grain for us. Then I'm gonna get him to put it into bags, so nobody don't get nosey," Johnny growled, puffing long drags on a cigarette.

The elevator agent wasn't willing to go along and get himself involved with us any deeper. Johnny got mad, roaring mad, and his face in a sweat, he lowered the boom on the bootlegger.

"Look, ya swine!" Johnny turned white as he stood up in the wagon to stare dangerously at the agent. "We ain't got much to lose — a coupla hundred in fines, which we can afford to pay. But if ya want trouble, ya'll be flat on yore ass without a job. So ya gonna play along, or do I see the cops and turn ya in?"

The agent's eyes bugged and he swallowed hard.

"All right, boys." He nodded and spoke in a choked-up voice. "All right — just cool off and be sensible, an' we can get along nicely, I'm sure. Come back in a coupla hours, and I'll have the grain ground and blended fer ya."

Things remained pretty quiet until we got the first heavy distilling done and delivered. When it hit the market, the police started moving, and folks got awful jumpy. Not that Johnny or I were afraid. I kept the money at home, buried in a quart jar under a floorboard in the corridor of the barn. As it turned out, the cops didn't even question Johnny or me, for I had cashed in my cheque, and nobody thought of trying to figure out what I was spending, where, and on what supplies. Even if someone had, the chances of pinning me were slim, for word was getting about that Snit Mandolin was setting his aunt's farm on its feet.

I saw Corporal Kane's car driving about the hill country, stopping here and there at farmsteads where he threatened or jollied farmers into telling anything they might know.

Kane tried other tricks, like cultivating informers to watch and listen for him. Tom Whittles was the first of these rats to show his hand. He'd been treating me very politely since the first visit I paid to his store on coming back — and by now I didn't mind him so much. I wandered down to his place one afternoon for lard and tobacco. After making out my order, he placed his beefy hands on the counter and leaned towards me, with a peculiar look on his face.

"Ya seen the way Corporal Kane's been driving around the last week?"

"Yeh — sure seems like a busy boy, don't he?"

"Well, maybe he's got cause to. Snit — the cops are worried about the moonshine they're sure is coming out of these parts. Maybe we should all be worried — it's givin' the district a bad name."

"So what ya think we should do — bleed for the district?"

"Oh no, don't get me wrong. What folks do is their business. But it's still terrible what bad likker does. Last dance the other side of town was flooded in the stuff, and almost resulted in a knifing. Corporal Kane told me so himself. Terrible, isn't it, how some folk will stoop for that lousy dollar!"

I was tempted to say something at this point, but changed my mind.

"I wonder," Whittles continued as he wrapped my purchases, "I wonder if old Dick Campbell has something to do with it? It's a dry year, and he's putting up a new barn. Doesn't it make ya ask where he got the cash to be so ambitious with his future as to be building a barn, and his bill here unpaid since last January? And his kids' asses bare to the sun for lack of clothes."

"I don't see where it's any of your'n or my goddam business what old Dick Campbell does at all!" I said flatly, and picked up my package.

"To be sure! To be sure!" Whittles blushed and lowered his head. "It's just that I was wondering — everybody's got a right to wonder, Snit. Folks have strayed from the Holy Word and good life something fearful the last while."

I slapped my parcel down on the counter, and clenching both fists, waited. One more word — just one tiniest remark, and I'll lay you out flat on the floor, I thought. Even with his head down, he was watching me, for he froze as he stood, not saying a word, not moving a muscle. I left.

When I met Johnny that night, I told him about my conversation with Whittles. Johnny blew his roof.

"If that lousy bastard don't want his rotten store to go up in smoke, he'd better keep his snout outa other folks' affairs — or he'll get what's comin' to him good!"

I agreed, and we got down to a busy night of work.

Business was booming, and all things accounted for, we figured on making about four hundred apiece to the good before the leaves started falling off the trees and we'd have to close shop or find a new location for our still. At least one thing we were grateful for — coming into late August, the nights were getting longer, and we could put more hours into our work.

We had to change our routine as well. For one thing, we had to dispense with Johnny's horses, because the marks of traffic on the blind road allowance were beginning to show, and it would be only a matter of time before the police or one of the neighbours would notice fresh hoofprints down a road which had never been used. So we began moving back and forth on foot, crossing over Rogers' farm, crouching low and following the hollows, our backs raw from the weight of water and grain containers. In the morning we would return, carrying the lighter load of distilled moonshine. The biggest danger we faced now was being seen by one of the Rogers family. Fortunately, Rogers didn't keep a dog, or we'd have been in real trouble. His fields were brick hard from the heat and bad cultivation, and our footsteps didn't show.

Yet I was scared, real scared, each time we came out into the open.

"Johnny — what if suddenly we should walk smack into old man Rogers or one of his kids?"

"Don't worry — they'd never talk!" Johnny snarled at me.

"Whatya mean — they'd never talk? Ya just tell me whatya mean by that."

"We ain't runnin' no Sunday-school, Snit — not by a long shot. We ain't gonna be nailed by no barley-chewin' hick! Just ya remember that! Now shut up and let's go!"

It was this sort of thing that scared me terribly, and I prayed to myself that old man Rogers would stay out of our way, for his own sake.

One night we were working hard, and both steaming from the effort. Johnny never changed his clothing, and with the way he sweated I was finding the smell of him as hard to take as that of the fermented mash I had to bury each night. So I called a stop for a cigarette to sort of purify my immediate surroundings.

Johnny went for the idea of a break. He rolled himself a smoke from the tobacco I carried, lit up, and crouched awkwardly by the fire.

"Pretty good, eh?" he said, and grinned up at me.

I didn't know what was pretty good to his mind at the moment, so I just grunted and continued smoking.

"Snit, I gotta talk to ya." His face pulled up serious-like suddenly. "I been thinkin' about the money we're makin' and how best to use it. Ya know, we gotta slow down some time, or that bugger at the elevator will lose his nerve and squeal or back out. Then where we gonna be? I don't know where else to unload the stuff, even if we didn't get caught ourselves if he threw in the towel."

"All right — what plans ya got?" I asked.

"Well, I been thinkin'; maybe you and I could toss in together and spend it on some — some investment. Somethin' that'll pay off even more in a few years. We could buy a farm with eight hundred, fer instance — or if we find someone who's really havin' hard luck, we could maybe buy a coupla farms."

"Yo're no farmer, Johnny — so what ya gonna do with a coupla farms — or even one farm?" I argued.

"I don't mean buyin' to farm. What I meant was buyin' them to rent or resell when times and prices get better."

I couldn't keep back from laughing.

"Who's gonna buy land from us here? Even in good times?"

"I don't worry about that none. How much ya think a farm pays in taxes each year?" Johnny kept right on.

"I dunno — forty, fifty dollars maybe — less if it's really bad land."

"So — we pay the taxes, maybe even invest in some machinery, and start raisin' crops that don't need rain every goddam day to grow. I don't farm, but that don't mean I'm stupid. What ya say, Snit?"

I figured I'd have to think it over more. It hadn't occurred to me that our moonshining couldn't go on forever, and sooner or later we'd have to plan our next steps. Yet I wasn't sure Johnny's idea was all that good. So we returned to work, and I dismissed our discussion from mind for a few days.

Every Sunday was meeting day at the church. Sunday was the one day of the week Johnny and I knocked off from work. We weren't religious — we were just tired.

"How long's it been since ya been to church?" I asked my aunt cheerfully over coffee. She looked at me with the expression of a person roused from sleep, but not wakened. I laughed, and she lowered her head the way she held it whenever she sat across the table from me lately.

A knock sounded on the door, and before I could rise to

open it Johnny walked in. My aunt did not stir.

"Hi, Snit!" Johnny was excited and his face was glistening. "Snit — I wanna talk to ya — come on outside!"

I stepped out after him and closed the door.

"Snit!" Johnny grabbed my sleeve. "Get some money — maybe a hundred bucks, and come on to church. I think we got a real deal on the go. I got gassing with my old man this morning — first time we spoke this summer, an' I learned somethin' everybody's been keepin' quiet about."

"What in hell ya talking about?"

"They's plannin' to close the church up!"

"So what's that gotta do with me?"

"You'll see. Grab some cash and come on!"

"I don't reckon Reverend Crowe is gonna be all that pleased to see me."

"Fuck Reverend Crowe! Come on!"

There was no making sense out of Johnny, so I went into the house for a quick shave and a change of clothes. I even buffed my shoes, which was pointless, as they would be grey with dust before I got more than a few yards down the road. My aunt looked up once to watch my preparations, but there was no interest in her eyes, for which I was grateful.

When I stepped outside again, Johnny was sitting on the grass, staring at the house door. He reminded me of a barnyard dog.

"Jesus!" he said when he saw me, but I hurried away to get our money from the barn.

Some people had already driven past and others were walking to church as Johnny and I made our way to the road. I saw Johnny's dad go past, sitting straight and severe on the wagon Johnny and I used for hauling whiskey into town. The Rogers family went by on foot, led by the father and mother, and followed by Mickey, who had grown into a fairly tall guy since I saw him last. Then there were the folks from the stonier land further north, all of them walking, for they were really hard up. We were not particularly sociable people in the hills. No two families went to church together.

"How does anyone go about getting married here?" I asked

Johnny as we walked with our faces to the parching sun.

He looked at me with surprise. "What in hell anybody wanna get married for?"

I laughed out loud, and Johnny stopped to stare at me. "Ya gone kooked or somethin'? What's the matter?"

"Nothin' — ya just answered my question, that's all!"

He watched me from the corner of his eye, shook his head, and didn't say any more. The road in front of the church was crowded with wagons driven half into the ditch, and the horses tied here and there to the fence. Folks were moving through the gate, and Johnny and I fell in line to enter the churchyard. I looked up at the church, with its cracked and dirty windows which were like the eyes of some tired, diseased animal. Reverend Crowe did not tend to the building, and no one in the community took it on himself to do more than sweep the floor for a wedding or a funeral.

Tom Whittles had opened the peg-and-strap fastening on the door, and stood to one side, beaming like one of those porcelain figurines which clutter every auction sale. Now Johnny and I stepped aside. We both had the same instinctive dislike of being crowded in a building. Whittles saw us and waved, but we both ignored him.

The Reverend Crowe arrived at the gate, and those parishioners who were still lingering in the churchyard hurried into the church. The preacher was dressed in a crinkled suit which had once been grey, but now appeared colorless and sun-bleached. He hadn't changed much from when I remembered him — he'd gotten a bit heavier maybe. But the eyes and shaggy eyebrows were the same, and his face showed no signs of further aging. He looked in our direction as he walked by, and seeing me, he stopped. The shaggy eyebrows twitched a little and he moved forward, as if to shake my hand, but reconsidered, and resumed a quicker pace into the church. Johnny and I followed, and behind us came Tom Whittles, still beaming.

Three years had not altered the preaching form of the Reverend Crowe. His sermon was a strong echo of other days, with his voice dropping into drowsy depths, then suddenly soaring with hellfire and damnation. He prayed for the destruction of sin — he prayed for everlasting life for the righteous — he prayed for rain — he prayed for a happiness on earth which I found disturbing, for it was so stern and barren a promise.

His words had an astonishing impact on this poor, superstitious and illiterate folk to whom he was giving spiritual guidance. They moaned and wrung their hands with agony when he roared at their sins, then a moment later they glowed and a sigh of happiness passed like a breeze through trees when the preacher subsided and spoke of the rewards of suffering. Then everybody sang; and despite myself, I joined in as lustily as the next person:

> The B..I..B..L..E
> Yes, that's the Book for me!
> I stand alone on the Word of God,
> The B..I..B..L..E

A ray of sunlight flashed off the collection plate which was now being passed through the front benches, with Tom Whittles standing in the aisle, never taking his eyes off it. I decided now was the time to leave. I was stopped in rising from my seat by Reverend Crowe slapping his hands loudly together.

"Brothers and sisters!" He stepped down from the pulpit, and his voice dropped from its dramatic preaching tones to an ordinary, conversational sincerity. "As most of you must know by now, we are experiencing terrible difficulties with this church."

I glanced at Johnny, but he was leaning forward, listening intently to the preacher.

"I do not wish to take more than a few moments to explain, so I shall get to the root of our problems right now — money! Brothers and sisters, we have no money, and if the collection doesn't rise above the pittance it has been every Sunday this summer, this will have to be the last service I shall lead among you. It just doesn't pay for me to come all the way here from town for the small sums you collect for me."

There was an anxious murmur from the body of the church and all faces strained towards him. I looked around, and realized for the first time how deeply ingrained was this building and faith in the lives of the hill-folk — like the homes they built and the clay they worked with a horse and a hope of some harvest. It was comforting, but at the same time it was frightening to me, an outsider.

"We just can't afford to give no more, Reverend!" a plaintive voice shouted from just behind me.

The preacher threw his arms apart and looked at his congregation helplessly.

"Then what can we do, brethren?" he asked.

This wasn't my problem, so I began sliding along the bench to leave, when I noticed Johnny holding up his hand to catch the preacher's eye. Crowe saw, and nodded.

"Well, Reverend," Johnny drawled, his eyes half closed and his hands in his pockets, "Seein' as the church needs money, I reckon the church should get money — whatya think?"

He stopped, and you could have heard a handkerchief drop in the building.

"What do you propose, John Swift?" The preacher was shaken, and had to clear his throat.

"What you propose? It's you needs the cash, an' Snit Mandolin an' I got it — how much ya need?"

I closed my eyes and leaned forward, trying to keep my nerves from churning up my guts. I felt every face in that church turning to me.

"Come on — how much cash ya need?" Johnny's voice was getting thin and angry.

"Tell him, Reverend — let him help us if he wants to!" It was the plaintive voice from behind me again.

I looked up, and saw that Reverend Crowe's face had become white and tense. He was glancing back and forth across his congregation, and I could tell he was scared of what he saw.

"All right, all right — we're still in meeting!" He silenced the murmur that was rising from the crowd now. "I think a hundred dollars would see us through another year."

Johnny raised one leg and placed it on the bench behind him. A little smile played on the edges of his lips.

"Tell ya what Reverend — we'll give ya fifty bucks. But since that's a lotta money, and seein' as anythin' could happen to the buildin' the way it is, Snit and I gotta do one thing to protect the buildin'." Johnny's voice was still thin, but now it had a trace of insolence.

"Fifty dollars isn't enough to —" Reverend Crowe began.

"Take it, Reverend — we'll raise more somehow!" It was Mrs. Rogers who now rose to give her opinion.

"Sure Reverend! Let's keep the church open!" somebody else called from the back of the building, and there was a murmur of approval.

Tom Whittles hurried to the preacher's side and whispered something in his ear. Reverend Crowe looked up at Johnny.

"What else was it you wanted to do beside give us fifty dollars, Mr. Swift?" he asked suspiciously.

"Well, Reverend, tomorrow I'm aimin' to go into town, an' I'm gonna buy a brand new lock, which I'm gonna put on that door!"

"No!" Tom Whittles shouted, raising his fists in protest.

"Sit down, Whittles! It's little enough ya done to keep the place lookin' respectable! Maybe it's time we got some youngsters to look after our church!" the plaintive voice behind me shouted.

"Yah, Whittles — ya was never put in charge o' this church!"

There was a real uproar now, and Whittles gave up. Reverend Crowe walked away, stopping alongside his pulpit, where he stood, holding his hands over his face.

A burly neighbour in front of me turned.

"G'wan, you guys — pay the Reverend his fifty bucks so's he'll keep comin' back! An' Swift, it's a good thing you gave Whittles a kick in the ass."

Someone behind me, rising to go, squeezed my arm and mumbled in my ear: "Glad ya turned out right after all, Snit. Maybe God don't forget some of us after all."

I felt both elated and weak in the stomach. Johnny bumped against me.

"Let's get the hassle over with!" he growled, "Pay that sonofabitch and let's get outa here!"

He pushed past me and I followed him to the pulpit. My hands were shaking something awful as I counted out the fifty dollars and gave them to Johnny.

"Yo're not serious about that lock bit, are ya, boys?" Whittles shoved his way between us.

"Here's the fifty, Reverend, I wanna receipt," Johnny said to the preacher.

"Listen boys — I wanna talk to ya," Whittles kept butting in.

"Forget it, Tom — don't make a bigger fool of yourself." Reverend Crowe took his hands off his face, and spoke to Whittles. The preacher looked aged, tired and beaten all of a sudden. He turned to Johnny.

"Whatever you're up to is your business, Swift. But one thing I want to know — what's Mandolin's connection with all this?"

"Snit an' me are partners, Reverend. Whatsa matter — can't two guys help out the church without you hollerin' murder? Or do we gotta try see about gettin' a new preacher?" Johnny was boyish as he said this. If he'd got himself cleaned up a little, he'd have looked like an average highschool kid.

The preacher gave both of us one long, hard look — almost a sad kind of look, then he wrote out a receipt on the back of a hymn sheet.

"Boy! Have we got luck by the tit! An' we're gonna hang on like two hungry cats!" Johnny slapped his knee with excitement once we were out on the road and walking home.

"I don't see what we got except fifty dollars' worth of friends. An' we need fifty dollars more than friends!" I complained.

Johnny laughed one of those good, long laughs which

brought tears into his eyes.

"Trouble with you, Snit, is ya don't look ahead. Ya gotta think big to be big!"

"What the hell ya talkin' about?"

"Ya'll see soon enough. Hey — let's forget it's Sunday and do some work tonight. I gotta get that lock tomorrow, an' I don't wanna go into town empty."

We had reached Aunt Matilda's place now, and I left him, saying I'd see him tonight.

seven

We did work that night — harder than we had worked any night before. When the first touch of grey showed in the sky, we had eight gallons of moonshine ready and crocked.

"Let's get outa here!" Johnny said, as he stamped out the embers of our distilling fire. We split the moonshine into two lots, four gallons to a sack. Then, hoisting a sack each over our shoulders, we left the bog and began crossing Rogers' farm towards the road.

I had no idea what time it was, but the sky seemed lighter than on any morning before.

"Christ!" Johnny swore. "Anybody on the road could see us comin', it's that bright! Run, Snit!"

Crouching low, we ran, following the beds of the faint dips in the land. Johnny was ahead of me, panting under his heavy load and the strain of running. I broke into a cold sweat.

"To hell with it, Johnny — let's go straight for the road!" I was ready to risk anything, just to get off the open field as quickly as possible.

Johnny turned on me.

"Ya just try it, ya yellow bastard! I'm gonna open yer

head with a stone if ya do! What ya so scared fer? Nobody seen us yet!"

We moved forward again, but I saw that Johnny was no longer crouching as low as he should have. Ten minutes later, we were in the scrub bush alongside the road. Johnny threw his sack into the centre of a willow bush, and then lay in the grass, his arms and legs thrown wide apart. I put my sack behind the bush, and then flopped down beside Johnny.

"Holy crackies!" he exclaimed, his mouth opened wide for air, and his eyes turned upward into his forehead until only the whites showed. "We run — we sure run! We musta run a hundred miles, Snit, I feel that tired!"

"What we gonna do with the crocks?" I asked, glancing back at the willow bush.

"Leave 'em there. I'll go home and hitch up the horses. When I come past here, I'll pick 'em up and throw 'em in the wagon."

"It's a lot of moonshine, Johnny."

"Ya're not just whistlin'! This is it, Snit — the big one! We get rid of this load, and we got 'er made!" His eyes swung back into focus, and he sat up. The tiredness was gone from his face, which became bright with excitement.

"See ya in half an hour."

We both rose and parted. I ran all the way home. At the pump I stopped to wash myself, then went to the barn to change my shirt. In about a half hour I heard Johnny's wagon on the road. Aunt Matilda was still asleep when I left.

We arrived in town well before noon. The streets were deserted except for the bank manager, who stood outside the bank, studying the sky as he puffed on a short, stubby pipe. He glanced in our direction, then went in.

"Just look at that guy — he's got all the money, an' he don't do no work," Johnny said sarcastically.

"Oh, I reckon he's gotta work for his living same as everybody else," I commented.

"What ya talking about? He steals, that's what he does — an he don't even have to go out to steal. Folks bring it in fer him!"

"Fer Christ's sake, Johnny — folks who leave money in a bank know what they put in, an' they know how much they take out," I argued.

"How they know? Who's so smart can remember everything in his head?" Johnny brushed his knuckles against the sides of his lips.

"I never kept money in a bank, but the way I understand it," I explained, "the bank gives ya a book, and each time ya put money in or withdraw, the girl marks the figures down, an' gives ya a count on what ya got."

"Like hell!" Johnny stuck out his chin like he was setting to argue all day. "They're crooked same as everybody else — 'cept they're smart, too. They don't run no place that size just to help ya count yer money! Don't give me that bull!"

"The way you figure it, everybody living runs a racket — there ain't nobody honest in the world. Is that the way ya see it, Johnny?"

"Ya gonna tell me different?" he snapped.

"Go to hell!"

I wanted to get away from his thick head for a moment. We were passing the hardware store, and I jumped off the wagon.

"Where ya goin'?" Johnny shouted.

"I'll see ya at the elevator. I'm gonna get that lock for yore church."

"Let's get it on the way back," Johnny called, but I ignored him.

The hardware store didn't carry any proper door locks for under ten bucks, and as I reckoned fifty dollars was more than enough to spend on that church, I picked out a strong padlock for three and a quarter. Then I made my way down the street to the elevator.

I didn't walk fast, thinking that Johnny could get rid of the moonshine and meet me coming back. When I neared the elevator, I noticed the horses standing with the wagon on the ramp, but Johnny wasn't around. Suddenly, I was afraid — afraid so it dried my mouth, and I started running.

When I got to the ramp, I saw Johnny kicking at the office

door.

"Johnny — what's wrong?" I shouted.

"The goddam, rotten, scum eating pig!" Johnny cursed in a high voice. "He's locked up — run out on us! I'll kill the dirty bastard!"

Again that fear — this time knotting up my guts like a bad cramp.

"Come on, Johnny! Let's get outa town!" I called, as I climbed quickly on the wagon.

"I'm not goin' nowhere until I find that rotten pig!" Johnny drove the heel of his foot against the door.

"Johnny!" I shouted, and he turned to me, his face white and sparkling with nervous sweat. "We're in trouble, man — bad trouble. We gotta get outa town!"

"Ya think the cops are onto us?" He tried to keep his voice low now.

"If they ain't, they're gonna be. Come on!"

I struck the horses forward, and Johnny mounted the wagon at a run. Once he was on the seat beside me, he took the reins from my hand.

"Now go slow," I urged. "Just drive outa town slow and easy, like nothin' was wrong."

"Ya fuck yerself slow!" he spat at me. Then rising to his feet, he lashed the horses, and we went through town and out into the hills at full gallop.

I staggered to the back of the wagon, and crouched where our crocks lay covered by a blanket. They were rattling against each other, and I was afraid they would smash. I began packing the blanket between them. Johnny shouted at me, and I looked up.

"If yore aimin' to dump the whiskey, I'll kill ya!" He was roaring mad again. "We're savin' our whiskey — ya hear me! So keep yore hands off it!"

"Cool off — I'm just coverin' the crocks better, goddam ya!"

Johnny scowled, watching me with distrust. When I finished and returned to the front of the wagon, he sat down and pulled the horses back into a fast trot. It was hot now, with the sun shimmering over the fields and hills, and not a breeze to blow away the oppressive air. The horses were lathering fast.

"Pull in, Johnny — ya'll kill the studs." I felt sorry for the animals.

"They ain't my horses — so why the hell worry!" he snarled.

I don't know whether it was my nerves, or whether some feelings had been building up in me for quite some time, but suddenly I had enough. Reaching out, I yanked the reins from Johnny's hands and pulled the horses to a stop. Then I dropped the reins and stood up.

"All right Johnny," I said as quietly as I could. "Let's step down on the road."

"Yeh — what fer?" he drawled, his eyes half closed.

"So I can kick the shit outa ya proper!"

"You! Ya haven't got the guts or brains to stand up to me!" He laughed hard, and began rising to his feet. But I didn't let him get up. I drove my fist down hard on the back of his neck, sending him sprawling on his side across the seat. He covered his head with his hands, and when he looked up at me, his eyes were big and scared.

"Cripes, Snit — what's got into ya?" The arrogance was gone from his voice now.

"Ya comin' down, or aren't ya?"

"I didn't think ya'd do it." He sat up and shook his head. "I never thought ya had it in ya. All right, I'm chicken — I ain't gonna fight. But I'd never do what you did, Snit — just ya remember that. I'd never hit ya when ya wasn't lookin'."

I didn't feel bad for having clipped him like that. He'd been asking for it since town. Yet we couldn't fight now — we were both too deeply in trouble to fall out. So I thought of making the first move to patch things up. But I never got the chance.

"Holy smokes, look!" Johnny cried frantically. I looked up, and saw Corporal Kane's car approaching us from the front.

I felt sick, and glancing at Johnny's face, I knew he felt the same way. I pulled the horses over to one side to let the mountie pass. But instead of driving by, he stopped some distance ahead of us, and poking his head out the window, waited for us to drive up.

"Hi!" he called. "You boys wait a minute — I want to talk to you."

He stepped out of the car and approached. I pressed my hands hard against the reins I held to keep steady, and Johnny slouched forward, with his head low over his knees.

"Let's see — do I know you guys?" Kane asked, glancing first at Johnny, then at me.

"You're the Swift boy — what's your first name?"

"Johnny."

"Oh yes, Johnny. And I've seen you before somewhere — what's your name?" He looked up at me.

"Mandolin."

"Mandolin — Hey, you're the kid got sent off a coupla years ago! I remember you. When did you get back?"

"I been back all summer — didn't ya know that?"

Kane grinned, and dug a thumb behind his belt.

"Was I supposed to know?"

I looked straight ahead and didn't reply.

"Your team?" he asked, indicating the wagon.

"No. Belong to Johnny's old man," I said.

"How come you're driving?"

"We take turns." The answer was as stupid as it sounded, and Kane broke into that laugh of his.

"Jesus Christ!" he said. "A couple of backwoods pansies!"

I cleared my throat and looked down at him. Kane's laugh wore off, and he hooked the other thumb behind his belt.

"Sorry, Mandolin — I was just thinking aloud. Which way you going now?"

"We're just coming in from town, and going home. What ya wanta know?" I asked impatiently.

"I just want to find out what's going on around here, and who's doing what — that's all. Anybody see you in town?"

A wild idea suddenly came into my mind.

"Yeh," I said, trying to keep my voice from sounding too eager. "Johnny an' I went in to get a lock fer the church — we're caretaking the old place now. The guy at the hardware store seen me."

Kane seemed satisfied, and began moving away. Then suddenly he looked up.

"Can I see what you bought?" he asked, his eyes narrowing. I shoved the reins in Johnny's hand, and reached under the seat for the package, which I opened to show the cop. He glanced into the bag and shrugged.

"Okay — I guess you can go. Oh — got anything in the back of the wagon?"

"Jus' some sacks to keep the wagonbox from rattling," I said, and held my breath for dear life. For a moment I thought he would go back to look. Then he turned and went back to his car.

"See you again," he called over his shoulder.

I never seen Johnny so scared and whipped as he was when Kane drove away, and we both looked at one another.

"That was good talkin', Snit — I never coulda done it," he said feebly.

"We're just lucky so far. What we gonna do now, Johnny? We gotta get this wagon back to yore old man — what we gonna do with the likker?" At the back of my mind I couldn't help feeling Kane had us tabbed somehow. At least, he was getting awfully close, and he could spring a search on me or Johnny at any moment. Whittles would certainly do his bit to help get us in trouble.

Johnny began to roll a cigarette.

"Snit," the drawl was returning, "don't ya worry none about stashin' the moonshine — it's that elevator bastard I wanna find now."

"He ain't gonna stash no moonshine on us!" I argued.

"Naw," Johnny lit his smoke. "Ya know where this stuff gets put? I'll tell ya — it's goin' into the church!"

"What!"

"Sure — that's why we gave money fer the privilege of lockin' the place up. I was figurin' on storin' our equipment

111

in there fer the winter!"

"Holy — Yo're crazy! What about folks an' their Sunday services?"

"To hell with their Sunday services! Ya think they're really so hot-up about goin' every week? Close up the church fer the winter, and by summer they got twice as much prayin', singin' and shoutin' stored up! It's good fer them!"

"But it's wrong, Johnny. We got no right doin' that to folk!"

"Ya wanna get caught then? Be different if a guy could get into jail for a year — learn a lot that way. But if Kane gets us with eight lousy gallons of moonshine, he'll fine us and run us outa the country. I got me pride, an' it don't make way fer no lousy, Bible-thumpin' hill hick!"

In a short while we were at the church. Pulling the horses off the road, we watched to see if anyone was around. The road and surrounding fields were deserted. I then found a stone to use as a hammer, and began fastening the padlock on the church door, while Johnny busied himself with lugging the moonshine crocks into the church. In a short while it was all over with, and I snapped the lock shut. Then I gave one key to Johnny, and pocketed the other one.

"That stuff don't stay in there a minute longer than it's gotta," I said, sitting down on the grass with my back to the building.

"Sure, Snit — soon's I figure out what that bootleggin' bastard is up to, we unload."

"How soon's soon?"

"Tomorrow — maybe the day after. Kane's hot, an' we gotta take it easy. What about tonight — we gonna brew some more, or ain't ya with me no more?"

"I dunno, Johnny," I said wearily. "I just don't know."

I was crossing the yard to the house, when I looked out to the fields and saw Aunt Matilda bringing the cows in from the pasture. I waved to her, but she didn't see me. Waiting for her, I pumped water into the drinking trough for the cattle and rolled myself a cigarette.

"Was you in town again?" Aunt Matilda asked as she came up to me. The heat was wearing her down, and she was tired and aged looking.

I nodded.

"Wisht I'd known — you coulda got some salt for the cows. They're salt hungry."

"I'll go to Whittles' store an' get a block of salt from him," I said. Aunt Matilda looked off to one side.

"Are you in some kind of trouble, Snit?" she suddenly asked. "You can tell me if you want — I won't go spreading it."

"Whatya mean, Aunt Matilda — what kind of trouble ya think I'm in?"

"That cop as took you away a couple years back — you remember him? He stopped here today an' asked where you were, an' if you stayed on the farm days and nights that I was sure of."

"Whatya tell 'im?"

"I said you was a good boy, Snit — that you worked hard an' never strayed where I couldn't see you. Whittles was with him, but he stayed in the car."

"Whittles!"

"What's it mean, Snit? Are you doin' something you shouldn't be doin'? It's Johnny Swift, isn't it? I don't wanna bother with what you're doin', but I gotta know what to say if the cop comes around again." Aunt Matilda looked at me with worried, clouded eyes.

"It's nothin'! I been breaking the law all right, but I ain't gonna be breaking it no more — that's fer sure, Aunt Matilda. First, I gotta straighten some things out!" I was mad fit to burst.

"Whatya gonna do, Snit?"

"That Tom Whittles — we ever done him wrong? You tell me — did pa or ma or you or me ever get in his way?"

"No, we never done anything to Whittles."

"Yet he been riding our asses Christ knows how long! What

for? He been fightin' us all along. We ain't fightin' people, Aunt Matilda — that's been our trouble. But after today he ain't gonna push no Mandolin around no more!"

"Snit — now you listen to me!" Aunt Matilda came after me. "Don't you go roughing him none. I don't want you goin' to jail on account of Whittles — leave him alone."

"He ain't worth going to jail for. Now let me be!" I pulled my arm out of her grasp and made for the road.

When I reached the store, I was all in a sweat, with my clothes sticking to my skin and itching me, for I had walked fast, and the sun still rode high in a cloudless sky.

Rogers was in the store, along with an old bachelor who farmed some four miles north of us. They were talking to Whittles, but when I came in, the two farmers looked at me and became silent. Whittles ignored me altogether, and with his elbows on the counter, carried on with what he was saying:

". . . wake up in the morning, and first thing ya do is mark another date off yore calendar — 'cause ya got no one to talk to, an' no way of knowing whether it's Thursday or Saturday. If ya wanna be a bachelor, Dan, ya go into business. But on a farm — nothin' doin'!" Whittles was saying to the old bachelor.

But neither Dan nor my neighbour was listening to him. They were both watching me, peculiar like.

"I wanna block of salt and some cigarette papers," I spoke to Whittles. He didn't move or look in my direction.

I hadn't counted on anyone being in the store. What surprised me even more was that the same folks who would have chewed Tom Whittles up in church yesterday were now on his side. I could see that by the look Rogers and Dan were giving me. I waited for a long moment, feeling a chill spread across my back, for if I gave ground now, I was licked and could think of packing out.

"Ya deaf or something?" I rapped the counter with my knuckles.

Tom Whittles moved his jaw slightly and spoke in a low voice. "This store is closed to Mandolins, Swifts, and all other kinds of cop-fearing, unchristian bastards who happen around here. Now git out and don't ever come back through that door again!"

Right next to where I stood was a pile of twenty-pound bags of rolled oats. I grabbed one of them and threw it with all my strength at Whittles. He ducked behind the counter and the bag struck the shelf behind him, ripping open and bringing down a shower of canned goods around him. The storekeeper came up with a scaregrin on his face, expecting to see me leaving the shop. But instead he almost caught the next bag I threw at his head.

"If I gotta bring down yore goddam store before I get service, then that's exactly what I'm gonna do!" I said as I let fly with a third bag.

"Hey, kid — smarten up!" Old Man Rogers lifted one hand for peace and stepped towards me.

"You keep outa this, ya gutless, crawlin' weasel!" I had another bag of oats in my hand now, but instead of sending it at Whittles, I brought it down over Rogers' head. He yelled and fell awkwardly to the floor. Dan, the bachelor, went out the door like a shot.

"Hey — help me!" Whittles shouted, when he saw Rogers rise to his feet and likewise head out the door.

"Ya still wanna see how tough and bad I can get? Ya wanna go tell Corporal Kane what I can do to ya? Go tell him — next time ya lay down to polish his boots. But ya ain't gonna push a Mandolin around no longer — no, no! You just ain't gonna push anyone around no more!"

I was wild with anger. Everything I had ever seen or felt that hurt or humiliated took form in this whimpering, scared man in front of me, with his back pressed against a shelf of groceries — his hands stretched out to push me back as I approached. The solid citizen — the self-righteous dispenser of laws — the detached animal, without nerves or longing — the untouchable.

"Ya wanna know something else, Whittles? Sure — Johnny Swift an' me are in moonshine — we made enough moonshine to drown everybody here. Sure — we're dirty an' mean an' bad clean through — an' ya know why? Because we gotta live! An' a man gets mean when he's gotta live an' the Lord don't provide him with nothing to work with. Now ya know, Whittles — but ya ain't gonna tell Corporal Kane! No, yo're not gonna tell nobody, because if ya did, I'd come back — sooner or later I'd come back — an' ya know what I'd do?"

"Snit — please! I don't want trouble. Let's talk this over like men." Whittle's voice was cracked up, and sounding like that of a kid.

"I'd kill ya — that's what I'd do!"

I was right on him now, and he sort of shrank in front of me, his head trembling against a ledge of the shelf behind him.

"Snit — for the love of God — don't! I don't care what ya do — or what anybody does. Just let me be — I'm gonna mind my store an' not bother with cops, folks or religions — whatever ya say, but let me be!" Tears rolled down his cheeks and he started to babble.

I walked out, forgetting about the salt and the cigarette papers. I was surprised to see how low the sun had fallen, and then this great tiredness hit. Like tons and tons of weight it settled on me, making my feet feel like they had grown into the earth for hundreds of years — that's how hard it was to walk. I was washed out — inside and out. No more angers — no more fears. I just wanted a grassy spot to lie on and sleep away the rest of my life.

Turning into the yard, I saw Johnny standing in front of the house, with Aunt Matilda guarding the doorway. I shook the weariness out of my head and began walking faster.

"Where's the salt?" Aunt Matilda called out when I got within talking distance. I stopped and stared at her with disbelief. It was her voice — suddenly so strong and vibrant, like it had been once.

"Well, where's the salt?" This time she snapped at me.

"I — I forgot!"

"Gimme the money an' I'll go get it myself!" She came

towards me, her back erect and her face sharp and alert.

"Or don't we buy at Whittles' no more?" she asked in a lower tone. "Ya didn't — mess things up?"

"No — no, we still buy at Whittles'." I dug into my jeans for some change. She faced Johnny.

"An' listen, Swift — if I catch you around here when I get back, I'm gonna take a stick to you — you hear me?"

That was it — she was mad! I hadn't seen her mad like this since I came back — and now, once again, she was the aunt I used to know.

"You know what he tried to do?" Aunt Matilda spoke to me, but glowered at Johnny, who had turned away from us. "He tried to move in on us! You heard me, Swift — say to Snit what you gotta say, then clear off!"

And she marched off to the store.

"The lousy bitch-cat!" Johnny swore, when Aunt Matilda was out of hearing.

"What happened to yore face?" I asked, seeing Johnny's left cheek cut bad.

"My old man did that with a piece of two-by-four. Snit — I got no home." There was an unpleasant whine in Johnny's voice.

"How come?"

"That fuckin' cop was over to see my old man — him and Whittles. That Whittles, Snit — he's out to fix us for what we done to him in church. He don't know we're in moonshine, but he put a bug into the cop's ear, and between the two of them, they give my old man a scare. So when I came home, the old man's got a two-by-four in his hand, and he says get out!"

"Whatya do?"

"I figured he was gassing off, so I give him lip, and started to unhitch the horses. Next thing I know, I get this two-by-four across my face. Jesus, it hurt! But he got it good, my old man. I knocked him down an' then I put the boots to him — the old sonofabitch! He started dirty, so I fought dirty, too!"

"How bad didya hurt him?" I started to get frightened.

"Most of his teeth's loose or out, but when I poured a

bucket of water on him, he got up by himself. He's sick, but he ain't gonna die by a long shot. But when he got up, he looked at me a long time, like he never seen me before. Then he says to me, 'Take whatever clothes ya got now, 'cause ya ain't comin' back.' He says, 'I'm gonna load up my gun, and when you step on this farm again, I'm gonna shoot ya dead!' He'd do it, Snit — the way he said it, he'd do it!"

"Great!" I said. "It's like we ain't got enough trouble already — now ya beat up yore old man. He can get you put away a couple years for that."

"Let him try! I ain't scared of jail!" Johnny snarled back.

"Sure — yo're the big hero. Whatya gonna do now?"

That put him back on the ground, and he started walking back and forth, twisting his hands over one another.

"I dunno, Snit. I ain't got no home no more — no place to go. I was thinkin' since you and me are together, maybe ya could fix it so I could stay with ya until I find somethin'."

"This farm belongs to my aunt — and she sure don't want no truck with ya. When she hears about what happened between you and yore old man, I wouldn't take no chances on yore even visiting here any more."

"Hell, Snit — ya can talk to her. Why talk? Just tell her that's the way ya want it, an' she'll listen to ya. Who in hell is she anyway, except a screwy old woman!"

"No, Johnny — we got no right pushing Aunt Matilda."

Johnny stamped his foot and turned on me, his lips drawn back like he was set to lace into me.

"I'm gettin' tired of ya, Snit — good an' sick an' tired! I'm gettin' so much of ya, I wanna puke, that's how I feel! Ya gonna play my way, or aintcha?"

"What's your way, Johnny?"

"The hard an' straight way. No turnin' around — no lookin' back! All or nothin'. I got no love fer no one, an' no one don't care about me. What I want, I aim to get. An' I gotta have a place to sleep and somethin' to eat, or things gonna start happenin' fast. Yo're the only friend I got, Snit — ya gotta help me, because I helped you!"

I didn't know what to do. I wanted to help him, but now

I was afraid — afraid of losing a home the way he had. Worse still, I was afraid of losing my aunt, just when I was so near finding her again. All this Johnny would never understand, for he had his own values on what folks did and thought — and this was the difference between night and day with us.

"I'll do what I can, Johnny." I spoke anxiously, because I had no idea what I could do for him. "If only ya can find a place fer tonight, I'll try and rig up somethin' fer ya tomorrow. Maybe I can get Aunt Matilda to see the score, and leave ya here for a spell. Hang on, an' I'll get some food for ya!"

"Bring it to the church — I'll wait for ya there." Johnny was watching me to see if I meant what I was saying. "I don't wanna face that bitchy aunt of yores again today."

I thought of something.

"Hey! Take along a hammer an' nails, so's if anybody sees the door open, they'll think we're repairin' the church," I suggested.

"Nobody don't see that door open with our whiskey inside. I'll wait outside the church," Johnny said grimly.

"Then let's pour the damned stuff out and forget about it! I don't wanna get no deeper in trouble than I'm in now!" I nearly shouted at him.

"What?" Johnny glared at me, and his lips drew back again. "Maybe ya'll want to forget we got gallons of mash brewin' in the bush, eh? Ya wanna chicken out, maybe?"

"Look here, Johnny," I wagged my finger at him, "I'm not goin' back into the bush to brew no more moonshine — no sirree. I gone far enough with ya in this, but from now on ya do yore own brewin'!"

"Why, ya rotten —" Johnny swore, his eyes buggin with disbelief. "What about the eight jugs in the church — ya aimin' we should spill those?"

"What else can we do now?" I argued. "The bootlegger skipped on us, an' with no wagon, how we gonna get into town? Maybe I could pull the two horses outa the pasture without Aunt Matilda knowin' — but that don't settle anythin'."

Johnny stared at me for a long while, dark circles of hate forming around his eyes.

"All right, Snit — that's all right. But I wanna tell ya somethin' — one day, you an' me are gonna settle. An' ya ain't gonna have no big fist to help ya, like when ya clipped me by surprise in the wagon. Ya ain't gonna have no aunt fer excuse neither, because I'm gonna settle with ya where I'm gonna get everythin' ready fer myself, an' in my own time — in my own way. Ya jus' remember that.

"Maybe I'll keep brewin', maybe I won't — I'll think about it. But them eight jugs is gonna get sold, Snit! If ya wanna help me, then we split like we split all along — if not, I'll sell them myself. What ya gonna do?"

"I'll help," I said, coughing to clear the hard knot in my throat. "When we gonna move them?"

"Tonight," Johnny replied.

"But how?"

"We gonna carry them into town on our backs, that's how. If we gotta wait a week at the elevator fer that pig to show up, we gonna wait. He an' I had a deal, an' he's gonna live up to it." Johnny's voice was menacing. He walked past me towards the road.

"Soon's the sun goes down, ya meet me at the church, or I'm movin' the whiskey out alone!" He spoke without turning.

"All right, Johnny."

I went into the house and sliced some bread and dry sausage. Then I wrapped the food in a piece of paper. It was hot and musty in the house, so leaving the door open, I sat in the shade beside the well pump, leaning my head against the cool casing.

I was tired, worn out clear through. Life was Johnny Swift — nervous and jumpy, full of hates and mistrust. And Johnny Swift was the hills — nice and soft looking, yet hungry as a wildcat. I was afraid of him, in a different sort of way than I was afraid of Corporal Kane or Tom Whittles, for those two had purposes which stuck out clear enough to see. But Johnny was a bit of everything gone wild. And because he was wild, I felt this evening I could no longer face the storm he was creating around me and everything I considered mine.

eight

Johnny was anxious to go at sundown, but I insisted we wait until darkness, to give ourselves the least chance of being spotted on the road. We had divided the moonshine into two gunny sacks, four gallons to a sack, with handfuls of dry grass packed between the crocks to keep them from banging together. Then we carried them behind the church, away from the road. After that I smoked, while Johnny ate the food I had brought, and we waited for the night.

Night was long in coming. Even when the sun settled behind the crest of the westerly hills, its red rays burned in slight wisps of cloud overhead, throwing a disturbing glow over the countryside.

"Jeez!" Johnny muttered. "Look at it — just like the world was on fire. It mus' be hot up there. No wonder we don't get rain."

I grunted and closed my eyes.

"Makes ya wonder about guys who fly in airplanes — must be screwy to go up there. Ya ever see a guy who been up in an airplane?"

I hadn't.

"I'd never do it. Makes me dizzy just to go up in the hayloft," Johnny grumbled.

The last bright light in the sky faded, first becoming a leaden grey, and then dark. A night-hawk groaned as it swooped down, and caught a mouse in the field only a few yards from where we sat. Johnny and I rose to our feet.

"Jus' one thing," I said as we prepared to leave. "If something should happen, like somebody see us or Kane waiting for us up the road, I ain't takin' no chances, Johnny. I grab the first rock handy and smash the jugs. They can't nail us with the moonshine spilled."

Johnny's face darkened with anger, but he didn't argue.

"All right, Snit — but nobody'll see us, an' I don't aim for Kane to catch us."

We hoisted the sacks to our shoulders and walked around the church to the road. My load was heavy, and the round crocks bit into my shoulder and back. But we had ten miles to walk this night, and I vowed not to speak of any discomfort I felt, and to ignore any complaint Johnny might make. Johnny must have felt the same way, for once we were on the road, we moved forward at a fast walk, neither of us saying a word to the other.

Whittles' store was in darkness as we walked past. Suppose the bastard is watching, and gets ahead to warn Kane, I thought. Then I remembered our row earlier in the day, and I felt pretty certain he'd be too scared to do anything, even if he did see us. He'd tell *somebody else* to go report to Kane — but time was on our side now. Three hours from now we'd be in town, and that would be the end of that.

Two miles down the road, my shoulder had become numb, and I was waiting for Johnny to suggest we call a rest. From the field to the left of us a dog barked, and instinctively Johnny and I fell apart to crouch in the ditches running along either side of the road. We waited for about five minutes. The next time we heard the dog bark, he was some distance away, and we both rose to resume our walk. We had shifted our sacks to the other shoulder.

"I could drink a well dry, I'm that thirsty," I said.

"Why don't ya have a swig from one of the crocks? The bootlegger pig ain't gonna stick no fingers in to see if all the jugs are full," Johnny suggested.

"Don't be crazy — I don't wanna die!"

I had said that as a joke, but I felt Johnny watching me.

"Snit, I know how moonshine's made — good moonshine an' bad. That stuff yo're carrying is the best a guy can brew."

"I didn't mean nothin'."

"Two years ago my goddam old man brought home a quart of real poison," Johnny continued. "It killed a dog Rogers had — bugger used to come and pee against our well. The old man used to shoot after him — never even nick him. So one day he stuck out a piece of bacon, an' the dog come. The old man brought him into the house, uncorked the quart of moonshine, and poured about a cup down his throat. Then he let the dog go, but he never made it outa our yard. Kinda dropped his head into the dirt once or twice, then rolled over an' died."

"Served him right — shoulda knowed better than hang around yore yard."

"That's not the point," Johnny argued. "It was bad moonshine — coulda done the same to a man."

"What — kill a man?"

"Sure. The old man took it back to the 'legger he bought it from. Said he'd turn him in to the cops. He should've, too."

"Whatya mean, bad moonshine?" I asked.

"Stuff's been doctored up — like a cup of quicklime to a gallon, or a dash of formalin. Makes a guy go hairy, or lay him out with one drink. Get enough of it inta yore guts, an' you'll go blind or die."

"No guy would buy stuff like that!" I was rattled by what Johnny had said.

"Sure they buy — guys who drink hereabouts ain't got money, Snit. They'll buy anythin' with a kick. If it's got two times the kick fer the same price, they'll buy. Ya ever seen a guy starved for likker?" Johnny stopped to shift his sack to the other shoulder.

"No."

"Boy, I'll tell ya, it's somethin'! They get thin and weasel-eyed, an' start shakin' so they can't hold anythin' in their hands. Then they get friendly as hell, or mean. That's when they gotta go out an' get booze quick. My old man gets mean."

"Yore old man ain't a boozer, Johnny."

Johnny laughed, hard and dry.

"He ain't, eh? Ya wanna go back and walk in on him right now. He'll be sittin' on his bed about this time, with his shoes off — spittin' on his hands, an' fingerin' his axe. Or maybe he'll be singin' his goddam hymns — that's just before he starts bawlin' like a kid with his ass spanked!" Johnny spoke bitterly.

"What about his church-goin', and dedication to the Good Life as he calls it?"

"Hell, Snit, he's been tryin' to scare himself outa the habit. A guy like my old man gets scared awful easy. He's a bad one — ends up by scarin' the hell outa everybody else, an doin' nothin' to help himself."

We walked in silence for the next mile. The moon rose, orange and warm. We could see the road plainly under its light, but it deepened the shadows of the fields and roadside. My back was beginning to ache, but Johnny didn't seem to mind. He was sweating a lot, and when we walked close together I could smell the heat and sour odour of his clothes. But he was like a machine now — just walking like he'd never stop.

"Ya ever felt sorry for your old man?" I asked — not that I wanted to know, but I had to talk to keep my mouth moist.

"I hate the bastard clean through." He said that quickly and quietly, like it never left his mind, even when he was thinking of something else. I didn't want to talk. I tried to figure out how far we'd gone — how many miles were left to go. I even argued with myself, like using my left eye against my right — why didn't we take Aunt Matilda's horses and ride them? Would have saved our feet. Or why carry the stuff into town anyway — seemed like asking for trouble. What if the elevator agent didn't show? All this for nothing . . . Then I would see the direction of Johnny's thinking. He carried a lot of money in the gunny sacks — maybe it was a risk, but one we couldn't take tomorrow.

I looked up, and in a field we were just approaching I saw a thin cow drinking at a trough.

"Johnny, I gotta get some water." I pointed to the cow.

"Hey — that'll sure be good! Be nice to dip my head in that trough!" Johnny exclaimed, and dropping his sack into the ditch, he began climbing the fence.

"Don't ya go sticking yore head in the trough before I get a drink!" I called after him.

"To hell with ya!" Johnny was over the fence now and running towards the cow, which lifted up its head, then turned tail at seeing him come like that. I tried to catch up with him, but before I reached the trough he already had his head down and was swishing it through the water.

"Rotten, bloody pig!" I swore, grabbing him by the hair and pulling him back. He blew a spray of water out of his mouth and laughed. I had to force myself to lean over the trough. When I did suck up water, I had trouble swallowing, for I imagined it tasted of Johnny and all the muck of his face and hair. Johnny was still laughing when we returned to the road.

"I gotta hand it to ya, Snit," he chuckled as he lifted his sack to his shoulder. "I didn't think ya was gonna drink that water at all. Guess there's hope fer ya to become a man like the rest of us!"

"Shut up!" I barked at him.

"All right — I didn't mean nothin'. Don't get rough with me — we got a long way to go yet, and we gonna need all our fightin' strength if we gonna get to town at all." He walked away from me. I followed, deliberately letting him keep in front, because I didn't want to row with him.

The higher the moon rose, the paler it became. Johnny still carried his sack over one shoulder, but I found myself shifting shoulders frequently now. Once Johnny turned and waited for me to catch up. I shifted the sack twice as I walked towards him.

"Christ — ya keep swingin' that thing like yo're doin', an'

ya'll get sore arms. Kinda looks like old Snit ain't gonna be able to make it!" There was a sneer in his voice.

"Go to hell!" I growled, and swore I wasn't going to shift the sack unless he did, even if it cut right into my shoulder. We walked, the dust rising to our nostrils and not a sound to distract us. I thought of things I'd seen and done, and then I didn't think any more.

"Hey!" Johnny suddenly called near my ear. "Whatsa matter — ya gone to sleep? Ya been walkin' like ya needed all the road to get where yo're goin'."

"Don't worry none!" I snapped back at him. I guess I must have dozed, because I looked around, trying to reckon how far we'd walked before I blanked.

"Another half hour, and we're there," Johnny said. His voice was tired. I looked at him, and saw the moonlight glistening off his skin. His mouth was open and slack with weariness. Grudgingly, I had to admit he was pretty tough when it came to taking a test this way. I had to turn away when he stopped to unlace his boots and scrape out the dust which had packed inside, for they had hardly any soles, and he must have walked the last few miles in quite a bit of pain.

When he cleaned his boots, I rolled us each a cigarette. When I gave him his and struck a match to it, I noticed him watching me with an amused expression in his eyes. He didn't goad me, though, for which I was thankful.

Reaching the top of the next rise in the road, we spotted the few lights of town.

"There she is — damn her rotten heart!" Johnny shouted, and we hurried on. I didn't ask Johnny what he planned doing. Instead I just followed him.

On the outskirts of town, Johnny left the road, and we made our way in a semicircle until we came near the highway which approached from the opposite direction. Here Johnny stopped.

"There's scrub bushes we can sleep behind, 'cause morning's a long way off," he said. "But I wanna be near that elevator when that sonofabitch gets there!"

"There's no place to hide near the elevator."

"We can go *into* the elevator," he suggested.

"Whatya talkin' about? It'll be locked tighter than a thief's house."

"Let's take a look." We moved forward again. There were no street lights near the elevator, so we came from the shadowed side without fear of being seen. Staying close to the walls of the tall building, we reached the ramp to the scales. The doors to the platform were lowered. Johnny climbed the ramp and tried the doors, but they were locked.

"Hey!" I called in a whisper. "We could hide under the ramp!"

The ramp rose at an incline from ground level to a height of about three feet, where it was joined to the elevator itself. Under it was a jungle of weeds and grass. Johnny jumped down beside me and peered where I pointed.

"Yeh! We could sleep like we was in God's lap. Come on!" Pulling his sack behind him, Johnny parted the growth of grass and disappeared beneath the ramp. I followed after him.

I dozed for a while, then woke up and couldn't go back to sleep for Johnny's snoring. I'd never heard a guy snore like he did. He lay on his back, his mouth wide open and his eyes only partially shut, which was pretty frightening to see. When he took a breath in, he groaned, and when he blew it out, the sound coming out of his throat was a gargle with voice to it. I jabbed him in the ribs, for I was sure anybody passing on the street would hear him. He only ground his teeth, and a few minutes later he was snoring again.

So I kept poking him, and hoping morning would come soon.

With dawn, the air became chilly, and I took the jugs from my sack, laying them side by side in front of me. Then I used the empty gunny sack for a wrap around my shoulders. Johnny slept with his chest bare and arms thrown wide apart. I touched the skin of his neck with my finger, and was startled to feel how warm he was.

Hunger was twisting in my belly like a living thing, and I rolled myself a cigarette to numb my appetite. In the cool morning air, the cigarette tasted impure, so I snubbed it out after one puff. At that moment I heard footsteps approaching from the direction of town. I shook Johnny, but his head bobbed from side to side and he continued sleeping. The footsteps came nearer, and I shook Johnny harder. Then the footsteps struck the edge of the ramp. Putting my hand across Johnny's mouth, I rolled over him and held him down. His eyes opened with alarm, and he reached for my throat. Awareness came quickly to him, and he relaxed. I sighed and released him.

The footsteps overhead reached the building now, and we heard the rattle of keys, and the heavy groan of the elevator doors being pushed open.

"It's him!" Johnny whispered thickly, his face flushing with excitement. Rolling over on his stomach, he crawled out from under the ramp. I followed him.

The elevator agent was drowsily unlocking the door to his office when we caught up with him.

"Hey!" Johnny called to him. "Been tryin' to reach ya — where ya been?"

The agent turned so fast with surprise the keys went flying across the scale deck, and his office door still locked. He was both mad and frightened.

"What the hell you guys doin' here?" he demanded gruffly, his eyes fixed on Johnny.

Johnny was good natured and smiling, fumbling awkwardly with his hands. But I noticed the nervous sweat beading on his forehead.

"Brought in some more stuff — been waitin' for ya all night," he said, stretching as he spoke.

"I don't want none of the stuff — whatever yo're talking about. Now get out." The bootlegger bent over to pick up his keys, but Johnny caught him by the shoulder and jerked him up.

"Whatya mean ya don't want the stuff? We got eight gallons fer ya!" Johnny was still smiling, but he was holding tightly to the bootlegger's shirt.

"Eight gallons! What the hell ya think I run — a likker store! Naw, I'm not buyin' anymore — I'm outa the racket.

You guys are poison." The agent tried to pull himself out of Johnny's grasp. "Come on — leggo!"

"Ya not buyin' anymore? Sure, yo're gonna buy the eight gallons like a good boy. Snit, open the door to this pigsty. We're gonna take our friend in, an' we're gonna find a crowbar and work the sonofabitch over so's his own whorin' mother wouldn't know him. Sure, he's gonna buy!" Johnny jumped behind the bootlegger, catching a stranglehold under the fat agent's chin. I grabbed for the keys and unlocked the office door. Johnny was already working him backwards into the room. I glanced out to the street of the town. Nobody in sight.

In a moment we had him in the room and thrown into a chair. I slammed the door shut. Among the litter on the dirty office desk which occupied a corner of the room, there was a tackhammer. Johnny got hold of it, and releasing the bootlegger, stood over him. Both he and the bootlegger were breathing hard.

"Now — ya still gonna chicken out — or we gonna have to work ya over?" Johnny was insane with hatred. He was spitting his words out, and by the way he stood poised, I was afraid he might just attack the agent without thinking twice about it.

"Cool off, you guys — there don't have to be no trouble." I spoke to both of them.

Johnny half turned his face to me.

"Shut up, Snit! Ya got nothin' to do with this — it's between him an' me! Look at 'im, shakin' with fright! Bet ya figured I'd get scared first after what ya done. Johnny Swift don't get scared away by yellow pig cowards!"

The bootlegger's eyes were swimming in tears of fear.

"I'm scared, Johnny — ya bet I'm scared!" he babbled, watching the hammer in Johnny's hand. "What's got into ya, man! I'll buy — I'll buy yore likker! Just don't act like ya was aimin' to kill me or something, Johnny! Fer Christ's sake, put away that hammer!"

Saying this, he lunged forward to grab the hammer, and Johnny swung to strike. I jumped in between them, pushing the agent back into his chair, and Johnny away to the table.

"Ya rotten weasel!" Johnny cursed, glaring at the bootlegger.

"Break it up!" I shouted. "He wants to buy, so sell the damned stuff and let's get outa here. If ya came for revenge, then I'm outa this. In fact, I'll go and bring Kane down here to straighten you guys out!" I said to Johnny.

That sobered both of them.

"All right, Snit — I'll leave the bastard alone. Go bring the moonshine in, an' I'll collect off him."

"No rough stuff?"

"Naw." Johnny was quieter now, and his face had turned pale and sick. "But I'm hangin' on to the hammer till ya get back, just so's he don't try no monkey business."

There was still nobody on the town street as I brought the whiskey out from under the ramp, and placing all eight jugs into one bag, dragged it up to the scale deck, then into the office. The other sack I left where I had slept with it under the ramp.

The bootlegger stared at the sack I had brought in.

"Take my word for it — there's eight gallons there," I muttered at him.

"Sure, boys — I trust ya!" He seemed considerably relieved now that he was in no danger of physical harm. "I was just gonna tell ya it wasn't my fault ya found the elevator closed the other day —"

"Shut yore fuckin' mouth!" Johnny's temper flared.

The agent cringed back into his chair until his double chins made two white collars around his throat.

"He paid ya?" I asked Johnny.

"Yeh, he paid."

At the door, Johnny turned and dropped the hammer on the floor. He stared a moment longer at the bootlegger.

"Ya can thank Snit yore head ain't bust in two, ya double-crossin' snake! Just remember, Snit ain't always gonna be around to save ya — an' I'll get ya then!"

"Why don't ya leave me alone? I don't ever want to see any of yore damned whiskey!" The man was actually in tears now.

"Aw fer God's sake, Johnny — let's get outa here," I complained.

Johnny slammed the door shut and we walked out into the street. The sun was higher than the town buildings now, throwing cool shadows diagonally across the white dust of the road. Neither of us spoke until we reached Elsie's place.

She was sweeping when we came in, but once we were seated at a table, she dropped her broom to the floor and waddled towards us. I looked down and saw that her feet were in a pair of heavy woollen stockings, with no shoes on. They were huge feet, with ankles that seemed waterlogged, they were so thick.

"Whatcha want?" she demanded, looking first at me, then at Johnny.

"I ain't eaten," I said. "I'd like a coupla eggs and some coffee."

She looked at Johnny.

"The same."

She still stood looking suspiciously at us.

"Ya punks really wanna eat, or ya just playin' around?" She spoke gruffly. "I ain't got much in food here, an' I don't wanna cook if yo're just jokin' with me."

"We're not jokin'," I assured her. "We ain't had anythin' to eat since some time yesterday."

"How many folks has?" she growled, but she seemed satisfied we weren't larking her, for a moment later we heard the crackling of a hot greased pan in the kitchen back of the café.

Johnny handed me the money he had collected from the bootlegger.

"Count it out, so's he don't get away with nothin', or I'm goin' back an' see the dirty, lousy —"

"Lay off the guy. We're finished with him, an' I don't see no cause for houndin' the bugger the way ya been doin'," I said as I counted the bills.

"Bootleggers is the lowest," Johnny said vehemently, as he leaned forward with his elbows on the table.

The money was right.

"An' ya know what's worse than an ordinary bootlegger?" Johnny was staring at me. I said I didn't.

"It's a bottlegger that tries to do ya!"

"He didn't try to do ya — he just chickened out!" I argued.

"The way I see it, it don't matter what the reason is — a guy like that gotta be kicked around some to show him who's top dog, I'm disappointed in ya, Snit — the way ya took up fer him."

"Whatta hell ya sayin! I didn't take up — ya'd a killed him if I hadn't stopped ya."

"So what — he's just a goddam bootlegger. You an' me, we work our hands to the bone, makin' stuff to sell. He just buys, turns around an' sells — don't ever get his hands dirty; an' I betcha he cleans up more on a gallon than we do! Then he chickens an' we coulda ended up in jail on accounta him. I don't mind goin' to jail, Snit — but not for that lousy bastard!"

"Sure, Johnny — I agree with ya. Now shut up." Elsie was approaching with two plates of food, and I didn't want her to hear our conversation. She plunked the plates in front of us.

"Now wot was it ya wan'ed to drink?" she asked, her arms akimbo.

"Coffee," I replied.

"I gotta pot of tea that's still warm, if ya wan' it," she said, and coughed.

"All right, Elsie — tea'll be fine."

"Youse guys is easy to please," she muttered, and made her way back to the kitchen.

Johnny cut a small part of egg with his fork and nibbled at it.

"This is good!" he said, and began eating greedily.

The café door opened just then, and I glanced up. Corporal Kane entered, his face drawn and his eyes sleep-angry. He saw us and came over.

"The cop's here," I warned Johnny in a low voice, but he didn't seem to hear me.

"You guys sure made it into town early this morning," Kane said sourly. "Mind if I sit down?"

"Go 'head — it's a public place," Johnny muttered without looking up. Kane glanced hard at him, but Johnny was bent over his plate, finishing the last of his breakfast. As Kane pulled up another chair, Elsie came around with the teapot and two cups. She placed the tea on the table, then looked at Kane through vacant eyes.

"Whatcha want?"

"I'll have a cup with the boys," Kane nodded at the teapot. Johnny took the lid off the pot and peered in.

"I dunno — there ain't much there," he said. Elsie took the pot and went back into the kitchen with it. Johnny grinned at me, then composing his face, looked at Kane.

The mountie was drumming with the fingers of one hand on the table, while he draped the other over the back of his chair. He was staring at Johnny.

"Well, what's new, co'poral?" Johnny asked with a straight face. "Catch any bad guys lately, or any moonshine makers?"

The drumming stopped, and Kane leaned towards Johnny. "Just keep talkin' Swift — and I'm gonna pull you in so fast you won't know what happened to you! Then maybe we'll get to the bottom of this."

"Johnny's only kidding," I butted in.

"You keep quiet — I'll talk to you later," Kane snapped at me. Just then, Elsie brought the tea back, also a cup for the policeman. Then she propped herself at the nearest table, and stood, with her arms folded, listening.

Kane turned his head to see her.

"That'll be all!" he said crisply, and Elsie backed away, her mouth slightly opened

"Boy — she's sure scared o' ya," Johnny marvelled. "Think she makes moonshine in the kitchen?"

"Where were you last night?" Kane asked Johnny.

"Oh, I been around." Johnny poured himself a cup of tea.

"I'm asking you a question, Swift. And I'm going to get an answer out of you if it's the last thing I do. Where were you last night?"

"Maybe I was home in bed." Kane was mad, and the cheek

was going out of Johnny.

"You weren't home at all. I've just come back from an early morning drive to your place." Kane began drumming on the table again.

Johnny had just lifted the cup to his lips, but he dropped it hard on the plate. His temples broke out in sweat.

"I saw your father," Kane continued in a soft menacing voice. "He's a sick man, Johnny — a badly hurt man. I could see you get three months for that."

"I don't care — I done nothin' wrong," Johnny blustered.

"And a couple of lashes," Kane continued, still drumming with his fingers, Johnny winced, and looked up at me helplessly.

"It ain't so — the old man musta done somethin' to hisself to get me in trouble! Ask Snit — he knows everythin'." Johnny was staring at me with the expression of a helpless, trapped animal.

"He's right, corporal," I lied. "Johnny was with me all the time. He never saw his old man."

Kane looked at me, and his lips parted in a hard smile.

"Maybe I can accommodate both of you, then. It would have taken two guys to beat up the old man like that — no one person would have taken so much time and work to do such a perfect job. You ever seen a man with one ear missing, and his teeth broken out of his jaw? He's staggering around now, trying to get his cattle watered and out to pasture. He could pass out any time from loss of blood. In this heat, he could die before anybody got to him to help. You know what could happen to both of you if he died?"

"Cut it out!" I tried to keep my voice down. "Why didn't ya bring him in for a doctor to look at him? Ya want him to die?"

"He's the same kind of person as your aunt, Mandolin — worked hard all his life, and hasn't even got a respectable shirt on his back to show for it." Kane kept boring into me. "Raises a kid to help him, and one day he gets jumped by one or two good-for-nothing punks who bust up what's left of his health. He can't even afford a doctor — you understand? And how's he going to eat with no teeth? Tell me!"

"I got nothing, same's Johnny an' everybody else in this bloody place! Why don't you leave me alone?" I argued desperately.

"You got nothing, eh!" Kane turned in his chair, "Look around you. See any other hill farmers eating in this café? Folks from over there don't eat in cafés — even a place like this. They bring sandwiches and eat on their wagons, or where nobody sees them. Where were you last night?"

"What ya aimin' to do to us?" I asked.

Kane poured himself a cup of tea before he replied.

"Well, I could do a number of things. I could book you in for attempted manslaughter. Or I could pull you in on suspicion of moonshine-making, then call in a few more officers to round up enough evidence to make a charge stick against you, or whoever is producing. I'm not stuck for ideas on what I can do to you."

"Then why don't ya?"

Kane put his cup down and thought for a moment.

"I've been here a long time," he said slowly. "When I first came here, you must've been pretty small kids. There was moonshine made and sold then. I've caught more moonshine-makers than I can remember — but there's one guy I've never been able to catch — the person who handles the stuff. The moment I start to move, he vanishes into thin air."

Johnny fingered his cup now, an ugly grin spreading over his lips.

"Ya tryin' to make a deal?" he asked.

Kane clenched his drumming fingers into a fist and glanced at Johnny sideways.

"I said nothing of the sort," he said coldly.

"Yeh, yeh — I know. But all this baloney about my old man an' the lashes — that's just talk, eh?"

Kane remained wooden.

"All right — I was sleepin' last night, but I wasn't sleepin' good an' had some bad dreams — ya wanna hear about my dreams?" Johnny's face was a study in excited treachery.

"Johnny, what the hell ya doin'?" I tried to stop him.

"Sit down!" Kane ordered me.

"Like I say, I was dreamin' — an' it come to me that the elevator agent was bootleggin' like a sonofabitch. Betcha, if yo're lucky, ya might find some jugs in his office right now. But like I said, I was only dreamin' — so don't put the bite on us fer nothin'! Ya know how it is when a guy sleeps bad!"

"Ya rotten bugger!" I shouted at Johnny, but he wasn't listening to anything I said. He just sat there, grinning like a satisfied idiot.

"Look," I said to Kane. "It's all wrong. Me and Johnny was moonshine-making, all right. He's got no call to —"

Kane was on his feet now, smiling at Johnny.

"Thanks, Swift — thanks a lot. If your dreams mean anything, forget I saw you. And you, Mandolin," he turned on his heel to face me, "keep your damned nose clean, or I'm going to bring you down to size so quick you won't know what happened! I don't like crooked missionaries!"

He left in a hurry.

I moved to the counter to pay Elsie. Johnny was behind me, but I didn't want to see his face again. Elsie took the money and stared at us through half closed eyes. Then in her wheezy voice she said, "If you guys got trouble with the frigging cops, then don't come around here any more. Ya hear?"

"Good old Elsie, the Borden cow!" Johnny said from the doorway and laughed. I left as quickly as I could, but not before I heard Elsie shout after us, "Punks!"

Out in the street, I stopped and counted out half the money we had made on the last moonshine sale.

"Yore share — ya rotten bastard — ya good-for-nothin' prick!" I spat the words into his face, as I handed the cash to him. He took the money without batting an eye.

Then he sort of slouched on one leg and said in a matter-of-fact voice, "You an' I are through workin' together, Snit. I done the right thing — it was us or that bootleggin' snake. But it ain't us no more — now it's me myself. Ya been goin' against me a long time, Snit, an' I'm gonna hit you too if yo're against me. Just ya remember what the cop said — keep yore nose clean, or him an' I gonna get ya into plenty of trouble."

"I see. Well Johnny, ya can collect the rest of yore money any time yo're ready. An' then I don't ever wanna have anything to do with ya."

"I thought ya was gonna fix me up with a place to sleep and somethin' to eat until I got myself looked after." I couldn't believe it, but he said that with sincerity.

"Ya got money — go buy yoreself some groceries an' set up housekeepin' in the church. Ya wasted fifty bucks of our money on that damned place as it was — so ya might as well get some benefit for it. I won't!" I started to walk home.

Johnny didn't buy groceries. He followed me, always a few paces behind. If I walked faster, he did, too. Then if I slowed down, I'd hear his footsteps become slower in the dust behind me. After the first few miles, it began to bug me.

"Whatcha followin' me like that for?" I turned to him. "Go ahead an' walk in front of me."

He was smiling, his eyes hard, but his face soft and boyish. He just stood there, waiting.

"Go on! Go ahead!" I spoke again. But he just stood there. I began walking, and I could hear him, still the same distance behind — still following at the same pace. My skin began to feel clammy, and pulling my shirt out of my trousers for cool air, I began to run. And behind me, I heard him run.

This is ridiculous, I was telling myself. He's got a right to follow — so forget about it and act like nothing was wrong. But I was getting panicky. Ahead of me was a broken branch lying partly in the ditch. Reaching it, I suddenly stopped, and catching hold of it turned on Johnny.

"I'm gonna hit ya — sure as hell!" I warned him. He stopped, smiling and scratching his ear. "What's the matter — ya forgot how to speak?"

He continued scratching his ear, and suddenly his smile broadened to a grin. Catching a good hold of the branch, I ran towards him. He turned and ran. I threw the branch, but it fell short of hitting him. I stopped, and he ran only a few more paces before glancing over his shoulder, and seeing me give up the chase, likewise stopped. His hand went up to his ear, and he began scratching again.

"Damn you!" I shouted at him. The sound of my voice, thin and metallic, alarmed me. What the hell's happening to me? I thought. I can't let him get me down. He's after me now for breaking away from him, same as he was after the bootlegger.

I began walking again, hard and fast until the calves of my legs ached with strain. And still behind me I heard Johnny. He began whistling — not any special tune, just whistling, high and low without any pattern or beat. It was a senseless, small sort of thing I could have ignored — probably had ignored, for he must have whistled that way before when we drove the wagon or made moonshine in the bog. Yet now it was a part of the heat and dust of the road. A part of the sun-scorched hills and dead grass around me. Even a part of the thirst which hurt my throat so that I couldn't swallow the pasty saliva in my mouth.

"Damn! Damn! Hell and damn!" I started to curse to myself. Whatever brought me here, anyway? I could have had a good job in the city, with decent clothes and money in pocket. Here I had nothing to look forward to — just an aunt who let me stay so long as I was needed and could make my way, a bad name with the police, and more trouble with Johnny Swift than I could cope with.

We were alongside the church now.

"Hey, Snit!" Johnny called, and I turned to him. "Ya gonna fix it up with yore aunt so's I can sleep at yore place? I gotta have some place to go!"

He was about ten yards away from me, and the white dust between us was dazzling. He was squinting at me, his mouth set and sober. I stared at him for a while, trying to figure if he was meaning what he said, or still trying to make a donkey of me.

"Come on, Snit — yo're not gonna let me down. I helped ya once!"

"Why didja tail me all the way like that?" I asked hesitantly.

"Whatcha talkin' about — tailed ya where? Cripes, yo're

getting as kooky as yore aunt, Snit! How about it, Snit?" I turned away, remembering what he did in the café.

"No, Johnny — like ya said, you and I are through. Ya gotta take care of yourself, and I gotta take care of myself, too." I started to walk away.

"Then yo're not gonna help? Is that the way it is Snit — ya become a yellow, double-crossin' bastard? Is that the way ya wan' it? All right — I'll get squared with ya for this. I'll get ya when ya ain't lookin', like I'm gonna get every sonofabitch who gets in my way!"

I put my hands up to my ears and fled towards my aunt's. Johnny was still shouting after me, but I didn't want to hear anymore.

nine

In the afternoon shade of the house, I waited for Johnny to call and collect his share of our money. Aunt Matilda brought me a cup of tea.

"Somebody comin'?" she asked, following my stare down the road.

"No nobody's comin'," I said. She stood around for a while, leaning one arm against the wall.

"Been losin' hair. Stuff comes out by the handful."

I looked up and saw her biting her lip with embarrassment. Her hair was combed back — severe and old-fashioned, but clean and combed.

"Say!" I mocked. "Ya goin' dancin'?"

"Oh, shut yore big mouth!" She pretended to be angry, and turning sharply, went indoors.

I waited, and overhead the sky deepened and darkened, but Johnny didn't come. I didn't worry about him — not in the sense that I was concerned about his having money. I just wanted him to come so we could divide our earnings, and part. I wanted no further ties with him, wanted the chance to stay out of his way and not create any great bitterness. I was afraid of him in a way I could not understand.

"You want supper, Snit?" my aunt called through the open door.

"Naw — it's too hot to eat."

"If ya want anything, say so now, or I'm goin' to bed."

I was staring down the road, watching closely to make sure, for through the shimmering heat of the evening I thought I saw somebody approaching.

"I been talkin' to you, Snit!" There was annoyance in my aunt's voice. A moment later, she appeared at the door. I was standing up now, looking hard down the road.

"What's the matter? Your eyes are bugged like you was seein' a ghost," she said, scratching the small of her back with a thumb.

"Somebody's comin'," I pointed.

"I thought you said nobody was comin' tonight." She followed the direction of my gaze. "Kinda looks like two somebody's comin'. I'll heat some tea."

There were two people approaching, but even at a distance I knew neither of them was Johnny. At the entrance to our yard they turned in. One of the men was old man Shnitka, smiling and looking sideways with shyness. He was hunched with age and hard work, and the hair straggling from under his threadbare cap was grey. When he smiled, his teeth showed as short, rotten stumps which failed to come together.

"Ay, Snit! Ay, Matilda! Good to see ya healthy — good way to be!" He greeted us some distance from the house. He almost tripped, he was that awkward and bashful.

"This here's some more of the folks hereabouts, Nick," Shnitka introduced us to his friend.

This man was a stranger. He was old, with skin crisscrossed with wrinkles, and small shiny dark eyes that stared out from under bushy brows. He had a thick, long beard of an iron-grey colour, and his hair was long, like that of a woman. He wore no hat, and the clothes on his body had been discarded by other men. In his hand he carried a violin with only two strings, and a bow.

"Howdy." He nodded, and giggled a secret sort of giggle,

like a man who's doing something bad behind an outbuilding.

"Nick here can make rain," Shnitka said offhandedly, then poked a long finger to scrape inside his ear. "Don't cost hardly nothin' — just two bucks."

"He's gonna make rain — fer just two bucks." Aunt Matilda mimicked Shnitka's voice and mannerisms. "Just like that — fer two bucks he's gonna make rain. How much flour an' sugar can you get for two bucks?"

"It ain't much," Shnitka said feebly, staring at his feet as he spoke. "Besides, everybody's goin' in."

"Everybody?" I asked.

"Sure — everybody down the line so far, except Tom Whittles, but Tom don't need rain in the same way us farmers need it."

"How's he make this rain?" Aunt Matilda asked sharply.

"Well —" Shnitka got real upset now, and swivelled this way and that on his heels. "Nick fiddles, and the rains come. Ask him — he made it rain everywhere else."

"Yessiree, folks — I can make it dribble just so much, an' I can make it come down in torrents — whatever's your choice!" The rainmaker stepped forward, talking loud, with his eyes closed and his arms thrown apart. "The secret's in my magic violin! Yes, my violin can open the heavens to those who wish it. You cannot go wrong. Up in the cosmos, something has gone wrong — the balance between good and evil had been disturbed, and it will take the sympathetic vibrations of my violin to restore the harmony to proper order."

"He's mad!" I said to my aunt.

"Can you make it rain, say right now — just to give us a sample of what's to come?" my aunt asked innocently. The rainmaker took exception to what she asked, for suddenly he opened his eyes, and quivering with anger, shook a fist in front of her.

"You are making it hard for me, woman!" he said in a rising voice "You are making it hard for your neighbours and friends — have you thought of them? Poor folks, suffering and crying for rain, and you stand between them, like a harlot in the temple! For shame!"

"Hold on now!" I stepped in front of him. "We didn't call for ya, but since ya come, ya'll have to show respect and decency fer us."

"Phah! Respect and decency you want! Just two lousy bucks, and you can share the good fortune of all!"

"Now now, Nick — these folks don't mean no harm. Matilda was just curious, she don't understand all there is to know." Shnitka sidled into the argument.

"Cripes, Snit — we gotta do somethin'. Reverend Crowe's been prayin' fer rain, and it don't come. Folks has gotta help themselves."

"Waste no more time on these heathens, my good man." The rainmaker dismissed my aunt and me with a wave of his hand. "There are other folk to see, but I warn you, these two have hurt our chances of a proper rain!"

"Now Snit, Matilda — let's look at this sensible." Shnitka was shaky and fearful.

"Did you pay him two bucks?" my aunt asked. Shnitka nodded.

"Then take your money back an' stop makin' a fool of yourself!"

"Ya don't understand — ya got no kids, Matilda. Even this late, a rain would still make hay of the grain, an' give us somethin' to keep our stock on. There ain't gonna be no milk at our place this winter!" Shnitka's voice was whining with anxiety. The rainmaker stamped his foot angrily and began walking away. Then he stopped and turned just long enough to lift his fiddle to his chin and play a few bars of a squawky and unnerving melody.

"That'll put a curse on your farm, an' maybe on others near yours! Don't blame no one but yourselves for being so cheap and reckless as to cross me!" he shouted, and made for the road. Shnitka still tried to argue, but seeing the rainmaker leaving, he gave up and followed.

"The nerve! Did you ever hear of anything like that? People — hell! Sheep show more sense than our folk," Aunt Matilda said with disgust, and went indoors.

All the same, I glanced up at the sky. It was perfectly clear and dull with heat.

Night was filling the hollows now. I waited a while longer, then decided that Johnny would not come, so I rose and walked to the barn and my hayloft bed.

I thought, as I tossed and turned that long night. I thought how pleasant it would be to live where a farm produced a living, where a man could work with a tractor in reasonable conditions and see plants which grew tall and strong. Where there was no more fruitless labour in working the soil by hand, or tormenting horses until they were just as weary and sick as the men who drove and guided them. Where there were proper schools, and a kid didn't have to begin working the moment he stood upright. Where there was no fear and no want to twist and damage the soul and body of man.

This wasn't farming — this wasn't even living. It was penal servitude to the blasted hills and desert-making sun; yet men clung to the soil like flies to a cadaver and wouldn't let go.

I had grown into the habit of sleeping late since working nights in the bog. Waking, I heard Aunt Matilda pumping water for cattle in the yard. Even in the shade of the hayloft, the air had the feel of being well warmed by the sun. I struggled to my feet and hurried down the ladder and through the barn into the yard.

My aunt was at the well, slowly working the iron pump handle and watching the drinking cows without interest. I came up to her before she saw me.

"Why didn't ya holler? I could've done this earlier," I said sourly.

"No bother — nothin' to do anyway. You could cook an egg in the dust, the sun's that hot."

I could feel it burning through my shirt and tingling the skin of my shoulders. Dipping my hand into the water trough, I scooped some cold water and rubbed it on my face and neck. It felt good, for a moment, and I came completely awake.

"You should wipe yourself with a towel. Your skin is getting dry and crinkly as everybody else's here," Aunt Matilda observed, as she again worked the pump slowly.

"Ach!" I grunted. "Just gets towels dirty, an' it don't make any difference. Ever see a cow use a towel after a rain?"

"It's been many years since I saw a cow in a rain," she said sadly. I thought of the rainmaker who came last night.

"Hey — what's gonna happen to the guy with the beard when he skins all the farmers and the weather don't change? I wouldn't wanna be in his shoes!"

My aunt thought about this for a moment.

"He'll hightail it outa here at night. But he won't really have to. You heard him talk — he could talk our Crowe to a standstill. He'll have something to say to save his neck. Never knew a guy talk himself into trouble that couldn't talk his way out again. Talk is a big thing. We never learned to talk, Snit — never learned how to defend ourselves, or explain how it feels to be us."

"I seen it happen even worse. Your folks and I lived close to North Battleford before we came here. Used to be a big Ukrainian settlement there. Those of us who didn't speak their language called them dumb bohunks — the silent ones. They worked hard, stayed outa trouble and lived on next to nothing. Then one day we heard that twenty young men among them — chosen to speak for everybody, themselves and us — had left on foot to go to Regina and ask the Government for better prices on grain and livestock, or else give us relief.

"We stopped calling them names after that, Snit — because it takes a lot of guts and figuring to reach a point where folks that suffer make a decision to speak up as best they know how."

"What happened to those twenty guys?" I asked.

"They got arrested for vagrancy and each got a month in jail. Then they came back."

"Then nothin' happened at all."

"That's where you're wrong, Snit. A lot happened — but I didn't understand it then. For one thing, the whole community started to work and think together — not like here, where one neighbour don't know another, an' every family is afraid of itself. They really got through — used to come together into the schoolyard on Sundays, and everybody would talk and argue about how we needed better roads, an' fertilizer for the fields, weed-killers, and all that sort of thing. Then the Ukes used to sing, playing their mandolins, an' the girls dancing. Or there'd be some good softball games. We were all poor as hell, but when you laughed it made it easier."

"Why didya leave — why in hell come out here?" I asked with amazement.

"I dunno — pride, I suppose. You see, Snit, in North Battleford, we suddenly found ourselves the outsiders — the silent ones. Twenty men walk away to tell the government who they are an' what they want, and suddenly you find everything you took for granted was just so much hogwash. It wasn't enough to stop calling them names — we would have to eat crow, and then run like hell to catch up, instead of standing still like we'd done for a long time.

"We didn't try, we moved to where no one we had known would learn how we made out. Your dad heard about this place, where land was cheap to buy and there was supposed to be enough rain and good soil. So we sold everything we had an' came out to Alberta. We sure got what we asked for, as far as finding folks like ourselves went. Jesus Christ, I wish I could die!"

"Don't talk like that, Aunt Matilda!" I approached to touch her hands on the pump. "We're holding our own against the weather, an' we'll do better next year. Besides, yo're getting healthier an' happier. I never seen ya this good since the old days!"

She looked up at me, and her face was so sad it brought tears to my eyes.

"Sure, Snit — I been looking better an' feeling better, too. I been fighting time to pay back for soaking up your money an' work. I can even stand back an' get sharpish with my neighbours for not trying — but it's all a big, foolish lie, Snit. It's all over for me now. You know what's the worst thing a person like me can do?"

I didn't know, and I said nothing.

"I'll tell you, Snit. It's to leech on — like for me to leech on to you, drawing on your goodness, strength an' sympathy — an' to go around pretending that youth was never gonna leave my bones, an' death an' the end of all dreams is only for other folks. Giving it a name — love! Then both you an' I getting sick of the word, but saying it every day to each other to make sure."

"To make sure of what?"

"Me to make sure you still respected my cheap pride, an' you to live up to your responsibilities — or what you figure are your responsibilities."

"Aunt Matilda, yo're talkin' nonsense."

She was still looking at me, fighting so hard against tears. Her lips were thin and trembling, yet she stood erect and proud, like nothing would knock her down — nothing she saw or lived through.

"I gotta die, Snit — same as anybody else. But I ain't gonna die easy. My conscience won't let me!"

"Ya ain't alone — I'm with ya. I don't want to hear anymore!"

"But you've got to listen, Snit — you've got to understand. Once you've made up your mind, there's no turning back. I don't want no love from you — nor any respect. As a family, we didn't do nothin' to deserve it. But you got to think — your life is too dear to throw away on a useless old woman like me, or a piece of hilly, rocky land!" She was pleading with me now, and I wanted to push her away from me and run. Instead, I tried to change the trend of conversation.

"Has Johnny Swift come calling for me?" I asked. She knew she was beaten, that I was fighting back against her attempts to open me to herself and myself. Rubbing her hand over her eyes, she turned away and began pumping more water, even though the cows had drunk their fill and were walking away to pasture.

"No," she said. "He didn't come calling. You're still mixed in with him, Snit? He's no good at all — he'll only bring you trouble."

Her voice was tired, old.

"Ya figure he's like that rainmaker that come last night?" I asked.

"He's worse. The rainmaker is a bad one, but he comes an' goes. Johnny Swift stays, living off people he growed up with. Folks who work got feelin's for one another. Johnny don't have no feelin's — he's like a dog gone wild."

I left her and went out to the road, looking toward the church. I thought of maybe taking the money and going to Johnny to split what we had. But the idea of going to Johnny, alone, made me uneasy. Besides, if he wanted his money bad enough, he could come and get it — damned if I was going to kowtow to him any more.

Aunt Matilda was warming a pot of coffee when I came into the kitchen. I sat heavily at the table and cradled my head in my arms.

"What you want for breakfast?"

"Nothin' — just a cup of coffee. I got a headache," I replied.

"It's salt you need, boy. Weather like this a body sweats a lot — an' if you don't put the salt you lose back into you, sickness sets in. You want some salt water?"

I looked up at her.

"Ya leadin' me on, Aunt Matilda?"

"No. Here. I'll make a glass, an' drink half of it to show you it's all right — then you drink the other half."

She busied herself preparing the solution of table salt and cold water. After prolonged stirring, she lifted the glass to her lips and drank half of it, passing the remainder to me.

"Here, Snit — make you feel like a new man. Ever lick on your hand when you been sweatin'? You gotta put all that salt back into you."

I took the water down with one swallow and almost gagged. She quickly came up with the coffee.

"Johnny an' I are through, Aunt Matilda." I told her. She was listening, but her face was bent down over her cup.

The salt water did cool me and cleared the mist from my head. As we drank coffee, I told her most of everything that had taken place — about Johnny's fight with his father, and him wanting to stay with us for a while. About the ratting on our bootlegger that Johnny did to the cop, and about making up our minds to call it quits. Through all my telling, Aunt Matilda didn't once look up. She just sat there, looking down at the table and sipping her coffee like it didn't matter what I said.

"Ya heard me, Aunt Matilda?" I asked angrily when I finished, for I wanted her to know I understood and was fully responsible for what I did.

"Yes Snit — I heard you!" She lifted her head to look straight at me, and I was surprised at the sharpness and anger of her voice.

"Well," I said, rising to my feet. "I'm gonna go out and close the pasture gate. While I'm there, I'll check the fence and replace any staples that are loose. If anybody calls, yo'll know —"

"I know exactly what to do if Johnny Swift calls while you're gone. Your dad's gun is in my bedroom, along with three shells which never got wet, so they should work!" She rose and getting hold of the coffee pot, walked briskly to the stove with it.

I stopped off at the barn to collect a hammer and a few staples, then went into the fields.

The fence was still in fairly good shape. In the dry earth, the posts showed little signs of decay. But the wire was hanging loose here and there, so I stretched and secured it against the posts, taking my time. Hot as it was here in the sunlight, it would have been just as uncomfortable for me in the house.

It got on well into the afternoon, and I was nodding, wishing I had a cap to wear, for my head and neck ached with exposure to the sun. For some time now I had been aware of a low hum in the air, like a motor running fast somewhere in the distance. But I didn't give it much thought.

Then suddenly the air changed. Instead of the soft, hot

breeze, a gust of wind came up which had the feel of ice in it. I shivered and straightened up, glancing at the sky. On the entire southern horizon, a dark grey bank of cloud was advancing quickly. The wind came from the same direction, and it was cold.

I watched, thinking with disbelief that the long-awaited rain was coming. Yet even as I watched, I realized it was not rain. The cloud twisted and spread, as if bursting from within, and the low hum I had been hearing now became a thundering grumble. The wind turned stronger and colder. I clutched my shirt tightly to my body.

The cows had been lying in the pasture, chewing their cuds. They now rose as one and approached the gate. In the other part of the pasture, the horses whinnied and with tails high also ran towards the gate. I still kept my eyes on the fast-moving cloud. If it wasn't rain — what was it? Instinctively I knew — hail!

The first pellets of ice were falling now, steaming where they touched the parched earth. Once I opened the gate the horses galloped directly for the farm buildings, followed by the cows, which ran in their fast, clumsy manner. I followed behind them, running as fast as I could, watching over my shoulder. About three miles to the south, the disaster had hit the countryside, for I could now see the wall of the storm. Larger bits of ice were falling around me. One piece struck my cheek like a wire whip, and brushing my face with my fingers, I saw it had cut my skin enough to bring out blood.

"Hi! Hi!" I screamed full-voice at the animals before me. They shared my sense of panic, for breaking into full gallop, they raced without hesitation directly into the shelter of the barn.

Turning off for the house, I had to cover my head with my hands, for the hailstones were becoming bigger and more numerous, and fell to the earth with a stunning speed. Aunt Matilda was standing in the open doorway. She was pale as death, and her eyes were wide with fear.

"Thank God you made it, Snit! I thought you might have fallen asleep — out there, in this — no one to help you or see you!" She squeezed my arm. Then she stepped into the kitchen, leaving the door open.

"To hell with what happens out there — the cows an' horses are under the roof, an' so are we — nothin' else is worth worrying about, Snit." She spoke with relief and happiness in her voice.

"What's this all mean?" I asked vaguely from the doorway, where I was still standing, watching the gathering fury of the storm. Aunt Matilda made some sort of reply, but I didn't hear what she said. With a thundering wallop, the hailstorm hit our farm.

In seconds, our front yard was a thick mat of broken ice, on which wave upon wave of other hailstones fell with a sound like that of breaking glass. A shred of poplar leaf, whipped along by the high wind, appeared out of the storm and stuck itself to the frame of the open house door. I looked at it, bleeding its green juices, and I was afraid.

"Will the cattle be all right?" I shouted to Aunt Matilda over my shoulder.

"So long's they stay in the barn, they're all right. Heaven help them if they wander out."

Then, just as quickly as it came, the storm was over. I stepped outside, sinking to my ankles in the sheet of broken ice which covered our front yard, the fields beyond, and the soft hills of the countryside. The sun had come out now. making the landscape blinding with reflected light. I was staring, searching for I know not what, hardly conscious of the cold wind which still blew, numbing my skin.

"Come in an' have some coffee," my aunt called. "What's happened has happened. No point in catching your death of cold out there. Close the door after you."

I came in, still too stunned and dazed to collect any thoughts into sensible order. Out there — a blanket of sharp ice, with everything that grew from the earth stripped and killed. Nothing left — no grass for the cattle, no hay for the winter ahead — nothing at all. I had never lived through anything like this before, and the fear I felt was paralyzing.

"How are folks gonna make out?" I asked dumbly, staring

into the cup of dark, steaming coffee Aunt Matilda placed before me.

"We ain't made of powder that blows at the first puff of wind. Folks have lived through all sorts of things — hail, blight and sickness. They'll make out some way or other. Who knows, maybe we'll get twenty lads to go see the government, and tell them we gotta have help this year. You're worried, aintcha?"

I nodded.

"We got enough hay to see us through the winter, an' you got money besides. An' *you're* worried! What about folks like Shnitka? He's got no hay, no money — an' he's got a flock of kids to feed. You think *he* ain't worried? But it's no use us tellin' each other our problems — we gotta act, or suffer in quiet." She began to mix some batter violently.

I couldn't drink the coffee, so I rose and walked to the door to look outside. The hailstones were melting quickly now, and patches of dark earth showed on the hillsides facing the sun. In front of the house, a steaming puddle of water was spreading from the melting ice of the yard and the water falling off the eaves.

The cattle and horses had emerged from the open barn, and with tails half raised were sniffing at the white covering of the yard. I heard a rooster crow from the direction of Rogers' farm, but otherwise there was a strange silence, broken only by wind and gently running water. It was as if nobody had lived here before — as if one disaster of nature could make the earth forget sounds of hammering, shouting children, and cursing, working men.

I walked to the barn to get some money from safekeeping, for I would have to go for groceries and tobacco as soon as the hail melted on the road. When I lifted the floorboard, I found the jar in which our money was kept floating in a pool of water which had seeped under the building. Not being able to find a better hiding place for it, I carried the jar back to the house.

Aunt Matilda's face dropped with surprise when she saw the jar and its contents.

"Is that — all yours?" she asked with disbelief.

"No, half of it belongs to Johnny Swift," I said.

"All bad whiskey money." She shook her head, without taking her eyes off the jar where I placed it on the table.

"It'll keep us alive an' eatin'. I don't care what colour or smell money has — s'long's it buys things. Ya know as well as I where it come from, so don't bug me no more!" I spoke angrily to her now, but she didn't appear to be listening. She was still looking at the jar, and shaking her head from side to side.

"I gotta go to the store fer tobacco and grub. Might as well take Johnny's share to him as have him tryin' to get past ya to see me here."

"You might as well. Johnny Swift ain't settin' foot on my land. That's more money than I ever seen all my life. Lotsa kids gonna go hungry because you got that money in your hands, Snit. You wouldn't have had it if it weren't for Johnny Swift. No, he ain't ever gonna set foot on my land."

"I would've had it, too!" I tried to keep from shouting at her. "How else was I gonna live? Sure, I woulda gone to moonshining, Johnny Swift or no Johnny Swift!"

"No, Snit — you wouldn't of done it." There was a sad, hard look on her face as she glanced up at me.

"Go to hell! Ya got less sense than I give ya credit for!" I turned away from her, and opening the jar, counted out Johnny's share of the money. I replaced what was left in the jar and handed it to her.

"Here — hang on to it while I'm gone. An' don't go spendin' it foolishly." My hand shook with nervousness, and I tried to sound joking, as if we hadn't argued at all.

But Aunt Matilda was working over the stove now, and paid me no mind. I stormed out of the house, making certain to slam the door so hard behind me as to make the windows rattle.

I stopped for a moment in the yard, watching the cattle and horses, which were restlessly circling near the pump. Then I looked further, to the scrub border of Rogers' farm, and above that to the bog and the hills beyond. Everything was grey and stark, and steaming in the low sun. The wind blew from the south, and I buttoned my shirt high against its icy bite.

The dust of the road had turned to a pasty mud, which crept up my shoes and onto my ankles. Long before I was anywhere near the church, I had to leave the road to scrape the mess off. Then I walked in the shallow water and floating ice of the ditch. It was cold, and my feet were wet, but I was walking faster.

The lock on the church door was hanging freely in its clip, and the door, blown open by the storm, was swinging in the wind.

"Johnny — It's me — Snit!" I called as I turned into the churchyard. There was no reply, and I hurried across the yard and into the building. It was empty.

"Johnny!" I hollered again, walking around to the back of the church. Returning to the gate of the churchyard. I studied the softened earth for footprints. There were none. He had left before the storm, if he had been there at all that day.

Taking to the road again, I continued to Whittles' store. The wind was turning warmer now, and what hailstones remained in the shady hollows were fast becoming water. All the grass along the fence lines and in the fields was broken and flattened to the ground. Shrubs were stripped of leaves, which floated as bruised bits of greenery in the pools. It was a depressing scene, and yet there was a feeling of exhilaration in the air, for the ground had been watered after many dry seasons, and the scent of moist earth was sweet.

At Whittles' store, I cleaned my shoes again before going in. In the dim light of the shop, I didn't look for Tom Whittles before closing the door behind me. When my eyes got used to the faint light, I saw Johnny standing behind the counter at the far end. He was eating from a loaf of bread and a tin of fish, which was lying in a pool of spilled oil on the counter before him.

"Hey!" I said, "I was lookin' fer ye at the church. What the hell ya doin' tearin' into the grub? Where's Whittles?"

Johnny's shoulders sort of sagged into a crouch, and his eyes were sullen and dark as he watched me. He continued eating, using his fingers to lift out bits of fish from the raggedly opened tin, yet never taking his eyes off me.

"I asked ya — where's Whittles?"

"He ain't here," Johnny replied through a mouthful of food he was chewing. Then he sort of smiled as he rolled his tongue over the front part of his teeth. But the expression in his eyes didn't change. I came closer to him, and it was then that I saw that his right shirt sleeve had been torn away.

"What's happened to ya?" I asked, pointing to the torn part of his shirt.

"Nothin's happened to me!" Johnny snarled, and particles of chewed food sprayed out of his mouth. "Whittles ain't here, an' I don't know where he's gone!"

"Then ya got no right taking over like this."

"Sure I got a right! I bought the store from him. From now on, I'm runnin' this place! Y'understand?"

He was telling me all this in a sharp, shouting voice, yet the amazing thing about him was that through all this he was eating, stuffing great wads of bread and fish into his mouth. A thought came to me suddenly, and a chill rippled down my back.

"Johnny — he ain't in there, is he?" I pointed to the back of the store, where Tom Whittles had his one-room living quarters.

His eyes narrowed and brightened feverishly.

"What ya drivin' at, Snit? Come on, boy — what ya drivin' at?"

"Nothin'. Only it seems kinda funny Whittles would sell on short notice, and then go away without seeing anyone. Ya sure ya don't know where he went?"

"No!" It was a tortured shout that seemed to come through his whole body.

I stepped back in alarm.

"Yo're feelin' all right, ain'tcha, Johnny? Ya don't sorta black out like ya can't remember anythin' ya do or say? Ya can tell me, Johnny — we been good friends." I talked quickly, feeling for the doorknob behind me.

His face had now become a cunning mask, as still holding a

hunk of bread, he began moving down the counter towards me. When next he spoke, his voice was quiet — too quiet to be real.

"Take whatever ya need from the store, Snit. I don't know the prices of things yet, but ya can have whatever ya need, an' settle later. Sure, we been good friends — come through a lot of times together, you an' me. Sure one helluva hailstorm, eh — betcha it flattened everything fer miles! Come on — take whatever ya need — act the same way like ya always acted before, fer Christ's sake!" His tone rose slightly on the last words.

I had found the knob now, and opened the door quietly behind me.

"I didn't want nothin', Johnny. Was just lookin' fer ya — to give ya the money we split. Here — that's yore share!" I pulled the handful of bills out of my pocket and threw them on the counter before him. He stopped chewing then, and the bread fell out of his hands. Momentarily, I saw fear freeze his face — the most terrible kind of fear a man can know. Then he seemed to get hold of himself.

"Like I said, Snit — take whatever ya need — there's lots of things in this store. Come on — take something!"

I threw the door open and backed outside.

"Ya don't hafta pay me — just take something like ya was gonna buy from any other store! Goddam ya — take somethin'!"

I ran like I never run before, through the yard and out on the road. When I looked back, I saw Johnny standing outside Whittles' store, staring after me, but he didn't follow. Still, I ran until I felt my heart would burst right out of my chest.

"He's mad, Aunt Matilda. If ya seen his eyes an' face like I seen them, ya'd a knowed he was mad. Whittles is in that store — either killed or hurt bad — he had no time to get him out. What we gonna do?"

It was getting dusky in the kitchen now, but neither of us rose to light the lamp. Aunt Matilda had moved her bench in front of the stove, and sitting on it, she rocked gently back and forth, looking at me and past me.

"You're sure you're not just tired an' excited — you're sure about what you think you know from seein' Johnny?" she asked.

"He was in a fight — his clothes is torn. An' he said he bought the store from Tom Whittles — what with? He didn't have no money on him. When I give him the cash, he was scared like I never seen him scared before."

"I suppose you should go tell Kane. Although I have no feelin' for folks who go telling cops against their own neighbours," Aunt Matilda said with anxiety.

"It's either gonna be me or somebody else. An' the way I see it, if someone else says or does the wrong thing to excite Johnny, who knows what he might do?"

"All right, Snit. You go an' tell Kane."

I rose to my feet.

"Snit — not tonight! Stay home tonight!"

"Ya ain't scared. are ya, Aunt Matilda?"

I could feel her eyes on me in the gathering darkness.

"Yes, Snit — I'm scared. I'm so scared it makes me cold all over!"

I had to have some fresh air to clear the numb pressure from my stomach.

"Go to bed, Aunt Matilda. I'll go close the pasture gate on the cattle, an' I'll come into the house to sleep. Then tomorrow, I'll go see Kane in town."

"All right, Snit."

The sky was clear and a faint trace of moon was showing over the eastern rim of hills. The air felt like the first frost of the year would come tonight. My feet were still wet, and a short distance from the house I felt the coolness of the ground seeping through the moist leather. So I hurried to the pasture. When I had secured both gates, I stopped for a moment to look around me before returning to the house.

It was then I saw the high sparks and flames from the south. For a moment, I thought it was the church, but the moon rose now, and I saw it outline the church just slightly to the left of the fire.

Whittles' store was burning.

My first inclination was to run directly across the fields to the fire. Then I became wary; whatever was happening, I had better stay out of it. Still watching the fire, I began walking to the house.

Before I reached the yard, I saw some people running down the road from north of us, carrying a storm lantern between them. As they came nearer, I picked out two men with buckets in their hands. Minutes later, Shnitka came over the hill from his farmhouse, also carrying a lantern and a bucket. Our house was in darkness, so nobody called in to take us to fight the fire. The neighbours passed down the road in the direction of the store, and soon the countryside and road were again quiet and undisturbed. I was about to turn into the house, when I saw someone moving in a crouch along the ditch, then turn into our yard.

"Who's there?" I called.

Whoever it was stopped, then straightened and approached.

"Who's there?"

"It's me, Snit!" Johnny spoke, and I gasped. The moonlight glinted off a small pickaxe he carried in his hand.

"Ya better stay away, Johnny — ya know what my Aunt Matilda said to ya!"

"To hell with what she said — ya gotta listen to me tell ya what kind trouble I'm in. Somebody's gotta know — an' yo're my pal, Snit — we been through thick an' thin together."

"Stay where yo're at, Johnny — don't come no closer!" I started to back away to the house, for he was near now, near enough for me to see the chalk-white outline of his face, and to hear his heavy breath.

"Ya said in the store ya didn't believe what I told ya about Whittles sellin' to me."

"I was only talkin', Johnny. I didn't mean nothin'."

"Sure, Snit — ya knowed everythin' — ya knowed I was lyin' to ya. Ya knowed Whittles was lyin' in the other room, dead!"

"No, Johnny — I don't know nothin'!" My arms and feet felt like they were tight against my body and I would never move them again..

"Yo're the only person come to the store today — the only person who knows everythin', Snit." He came a step nearer, but now he was crouching like he was aiming to jump at me.

"I told my aunt," I said out of despair.

"Ya told the kook? Ya shouldn't a done that, Snit — she didn't like me none, but she never done me dirt nohow. Ya wanna hear what happened?"

"No!" I cried. Another step — how many more before I had my back against the wall of the house?

"I was in his store," Johnny spoke quickly now, his voice thick and heavy with some inner passion. "An' this storm come up. I was tryin' to get some grub an' tobacco on credit — an' Whittles won't give me none. Says I'd never get credit in his store. Then he tells me to get out. Ya hear me, Snit — he pushed me an' I fell. Then he come at me with his boot — that's the livin' truth, he did!

"I got to my feet and grabbed this barrel pick off the counter. He didn't see me holdin' it, an' when he come at me, I hit him across the head. He jus' fell an' never come up. I was gonna go out an' run so nobody'd ever catch me, but this hail was outside. So I waited, draggin' Whittles into his room. I tried to close his eyes from lookin' — but they wouldn't stay closed! He jus' kept them open fer mean, the dirty sonofabitch!"

"Stop it, Johnny!" I tried to keep the panic I felt out of my voice. "Let's be friends an' forget about it — forget we seen each other tonight!"

"It ain't hard to kill a man, Snit — only ya gotta run or bury the dead. Ya can't live in the same place as the man ya kill. I tried to close his eyes — but they won't stop lookin' — only he don't see nothin'!"

"Johnny, yo're sick! Leave me alone!"

"Ya ever see a dead man — an' knowin' ya made him that way? It makes ya short of breath, ya feel that good — an' then the creeps sets in."

"Johnny — no!"

162

"I gotta kill ya, Snit — or I'll never know what ya'd do when ya got the chance."

"For the love of God!" I could retreat no further. My back was against the wall of the house, and I sucked my body into my spine to make myself as small as possible. Johnny approached, slowly inching his way with his feet, the pick held ready before his face.

As if through a set of senses other than my own, I heard the muffled explosion and the splinter of glass. As if through another set of eyes, I saw Johnny grow rigid, then straighten with the poised, slow movements of a diver under water. His head went back, and his mouth opened in a silent cry of agony. Then he fell.

It seemed a long time later when I mustered enough courage to bend over him and feel for a heartbeat in his chest. He was dead. Behind me, the lamp flared and lit in the kitchen. I looked up through the shattered slivers of window glass and saw my aunt, still holding my father's rifle, standing erect before the kitchen table, and weeping.

"Have a good cry, Aunt Matilda — cry for both of us, because we gotta cry a lot if we gonna live," I said as I took her in my arms, gun and all.

Still later in that moment which is the heart of all mortal time, I heard footsteps and voices outside.

"What the hell's happened here? Jesus, Jesus! It's the Swift boy! Who's gonna get the cops?"

"It's all right — Shnitka's gone to tell Kane about Whittles."

"Don't touch nothin' — just leave everythin' as it is!"

Then the door was pushed open and footsteps came over our threshold.

"What about those two?"

"Leave 'em alone — they can talk to the cops — we got no more business here!"

"What a helluva night — Jesus, Jesus!"

The footsteps and voices departed. Aunt Matilda and I were left alone again.

TALONBOOKS — FICTION IN PRINT 1977

Songs My Mother Taught Me — Audrey Thomas
Blown Figures — Audrey Thomas
Hungry Hills — George Ryga
Theme for Diverse Instruments — Jane Rule
Mrs. Blood — Audrey Thomas
Night Desk — George Ryga
Ballad of a Stonepicker — George Ryga
Dürer's Angel — Marie-Claire Blais
A Short Sad Book — George Bowering
Desert of the Heart — Jane Rule
The School-Marm Tree — Howard O'Hagan
The Woman Who Got on at Jasper Station — Howard O'Hagan